The Cheat

AMY GOLDMAN KOSS

SCHOLASTIC INC.

New York Toronto London Auckland Sydney
Mexico City New Delhi Hong Kong Buenos Aires

To Mr. Hoodie and Ms. Loo

ISBN 0-439-69945-2

12 11 10 9 8 7 6 5 4 3 2   4 5 6 7 8 9/0

Printed in the U.S.A.   40

First Scholastic printing, October 2004

Designed by Kimi Weart
Text set in Carmina
Many thanks to Lauri Hornik, Susan Cohen, Susan Silk, and Barry Goldman,
without whom these pages would still be trees.
Love, AGK

Friday

Sarah

When it all began
    I had no idea
        anything was beginning.
  I just thought it was *sweet* that a guy I barely knew brought me the midterm answers out of the blue.

  Thanks to his gallantry, I wouldn't have to spend time cramming for the geography exam. Less time memorizing geographic factoids left more time for me to
    cure AIDS,
        and discover a triple-acting defense
        against poverty,
        terrorism,
        and pizza breath.
    Well,
    actually,
        less time studying
            just meant

                    more time
                    not studying.
But the gift of free time is nothing to sneeze at. It sure beat
flowers, or sickly scented bath salts or other
                    Gooney
                    Gifts
                    Guys
                    Give
                    Girls.
Nonetheless, having not the least interest in this boy, I didn't
give his generosity much thought at the time. If anyone had
told me that his delivering a piece of paper to me would be
the start of anything even the tiniest bit significant in my life,
                    I would've said, "right,"
                    meaning wrong.
                    I would have said, "la,"
                    meaning nah.
                    Or
                    I wouldn't have
                    bothered
                    to
                    grunt.

Katie

Mr. White gave me a squinty look when he handed out the geography exams. Now I feel his eyeballs rolling up and down my neck. Cold, clammy, suspicious eyeballs.

But even if he WERE watching me (which he's not), all he'd see is a nervous eighth grader getting ready to take her mid-term. Nothing peculiar about that, right?

Even if he saw a GUILTY-looking eighth grader (with arrows beaming down at her and the word CHEATER flashing in lights over her head), it STILL wouldn't prove anything.

And even if he could read my mind (which he can't), all he'd see would be a list of letters: A, A, C, B, C . . .

Maybe he'd hear my song: to the tune of "Row, Row, Row Your Boat" (sort of).

Animal, animal, cat, boy, cat,
Cat, cat, boy, cat, animal.
Cat, cat, animal, cat, boy, cat,
Animal, animal, boy.

7

Mr. White the mind-reader would find it pretty suspicious if the same song were running through Sarah's brain. Good thing she decided not to set hers to music. She said she remembers poems easier than songs.

I don't know who else she gave the answers to. But even if she handed them out to every kid in class, they can't ALL be using "Row, Row, Row Your Boat." Probably "Twinkle, Twinkle" is more popular . . . or "Three Blind Mice."

Just sitting here staring at the test is NOT doing me any good. I have got to pick up the pencil and have at it.

Okay, Katie. Let's go. Mark the first A. (Animal. Animal. Cat. Boy. Cat.)

I cannot believe what a chicken I am.

I feel Mr. White's eyes—now they're hot and pointy—burrowing into my skull.

Two, three, four . . . (I am not going to look at him until I reach ten.)

. . . Nine. Nope. He's not even looking in this direction.

How about my dad? Is he watching? I'm embarrassed to even ASK myself such a question, because if heaven is so dull that there's nothing better to do than watch your kid take a geography test—then why bother to be good enough to go there?

Oh, NOW I'm really sinking into stupidity.

Meanwhile, as I dither away, minutes slip by, and Mr. White is watching the clock.

"KATIE!" I tell myself. "I order you to pick up your pencil and begin cheating at once!"

I wonder what Mr. White would do if he caught me. When

Stu Roper was caught with a cheat sheet in the beginning of the year, Mr. White made him take the quiz all by himself after school. That's not so terrible. I mean, I'd be humiliated to the BONE, but I don't think I'd have to shoot myself.

That was only a unit quiz, though. Not a midterm. There's no telling WHAT he'd do to a midterm cheater.

I can't do it. I can't do it because: A) I just can't. B) It's making me sick. C) It's making me crazy.

But how do I NOT? The song is right here, unignorable, rowing around in my head. Animal, animal, cat, boy, cat . . .

I know. I'll do the problems out of order. Just pick one and answer it. Then jump around and read another one.

Okay. Number five: The La Paz River. . .

9

Rob

Must be how it feels to be smart. Answers line up in my mind—like little kids for pony rides. Easy as ABC. Actually, AACB.

Know what to mark without even reading the question. Number one, A. Number two, A again.

That song "If it weren't for bad luck, I'd have no luck at all"? Well, taking this test is changing my luck.

Done before practically everyone. Don't want to look suspicious. Usually I'm one of the last. Or I'm the kid who has to have the test ripped out from under him. Not today. Feeling good. Stretch, yawn, look around at the poor fools still sweating away.

Kill time, pretend to check my work. Then I read: The La Paz River runs between A) Nepal and India, B) El Salvador and Guatemala, C) Iraq and Iran.

Trickle of ice water down my spine. Don't know squat about geography, but *do* know the Rio de la Paz runs between

El Salvador and Guatemala. *Ought* to know—that's where my dad was stationed in the Army.

Why'd I mark C instead of B?

Quickly correct the river answer. But if *that* answer's wrong, how many others are? Ice water turns to icicles—brain freezes. Read the other questions. Test translates into some bizarre language. Jumbled alphabet makes no sense. Gouge at the paper, scrub out random answers, erase so hard, the paper rips. Then change the answers back.

Panic. Do I turn this in and flunk? Crumple it up? Tell Mr. White I'm sick?

Yes! Go to the nurse. Study like mad over the weekend, retest next week.

But Mr. White clears his throat. Too late. The gig is up.

Ruby

Well, last night Danny was such a pain that I was all, "Fine. Leave. Whatever."

I mean, did he think I was about to . . . what? *Beg?*

But he goes, "No, no, really, man, I'm sorry." (Can you *stand* that he calls me *man?*) He says something about having a huge, like, geography test tomorrow and he hasn't studied, and I'm thinking, "Excuse me, but whose fault is that?" He had as much time to study for it as anybody else in his class. Am I right?

Then I guess he notices I'm not exactly gushing with, like, sympathy, so he stops whining and tries to act semi-human. But still, you'd have to be, like, in a coma not to see that he was, I don't know, mad or whatever. And it was *embarrassing.* I mean, there we were, supposedly *helping* and it was supposed to be romantic and all like that, and there's Danny, the grump, just sort of moving chairs around, with a fish face.

Actually, my sister was so, like, *out there* that she probably didn't notice Danny, because it's *her* engagement party and *her* everything: her guests, her seating arrangements . . .

And my parents are, like, "Will the caterers screw up?" "Will the weather stink?" "Will the centerpieces look stupid?" So maybe no one noticed Danny being so, you know, whatever. But *I* sure noticed, and ask me if I liked it.

Then, finally I, like, *repeat*, "Okay, just *leave* then, Danny," figuring he'll get it that I'm seriously ticked.

But he starts nodding and backing away and, like, *thanking* me, and says he's *really* gotta study for that test or whatever.

And I go, "So who's stopping you?" (Never mind that he promised like a million weeks ago that he'd help us set up.)

So he just left! Like, actually *left*! Good-bye!

And I'm all, like, "Fine," and thinking, in that case, he might as well just forget my sister's party, too!

Okay, so then I see Danny this morning before school and he's all, like, friendly. Saying he's *sorry* for being in such a snit last night. Now he's all smiles, and I'm, like—*not*.

So he goes, "Don't be mad," and I can tell he's practically *dying* to tell me something. But I'm, like, not playing.

This drives him bonkers so he's all, "Wanna know why I'm not dead tired from studying all night?"

So I go, like, "No."

And he says something about Sarah helping him out, or Sarah saving his butt, or whatever. And I think, *Sarah?* Excuse me? *Sarah Collier???* He left me dragging chairs around while he went to study with Sarah Collier? And I'm, what? Supposed to be *happy* for him?

13

So I spin around to split and I say, "Fine," or whatever. But my heart's goin' nuts and my face is probably, like, beet red.

I just cannot believe he broke up with me like that! With that stupid *grin* on his face. The day before my sister's engagement luncheon when my whole entire family thinks he's coming and that he's, like, my date and *boyfriend*. And they're going to *ask* me, "Where's *Danny*? Why isn't *Danny* here?" And I'm supposed to say . . . what? That he dumped me for *Sarah*???

So I'm walking away and he grabs my arm and goes, "What are you getting all bent about?"

And I go, like . . . I don't say anything.

And the bell rings and I leave, and he's all like, "Huh?"

And I am totally *not* crying, but it takes every drop of my strength.

Ask me if I need this.

Rob

Grab Dan in the hall. Say, "We're totally screwed." But he thinks I'm just paranoid. Says, "Lighten up and enjoy!"

Enjoy what? Flunking?

Tell him that when my old man has a few beers he starts on the Rio de la Paz stories. So I *know* the river answer's dead wrong. Dan interrupts, says it's brilliant to have a few wrong answers. Makes it seem more natural. He says everything's cool.

Sarah

I was minding my own business in American Lit. when the intercom hissed and the school secretary's voice quackled into the room.

"Would Sawa Colliea, Wobbit King, and Daniel Bwand pwease wepowt to the pwincipal's office?"

Her Elmer Fudd thing usually cracks me up. But not today. Today's cracks, hearing her string my name with theirs, were the chipping and shattering, not the tee-hee kind.

"Run!" said the little brain.

"Run! Hide! Deny!"

"Too late," said the bigger brain.

"Too late to even try."

Everyone turned to watch me gather my books. Getting my breathing under control took a beat, but when I was sure my knees wouldn't knock, I got up and swanned down the row of desks. Neck arched, wings poised. (Ugly feet hidden underwater.)

I even put a smile on my beak on the way out:
As if to say, "I wonder *what* this could be about?"
As if to say, "Perhaps they want to give me an award,
a shiny trophy with a cash prize,
and a chance to appear
on a game show!"
As if to say, "Called to the office? Me? Oh dear!
I hope my family and pets are all right.
I hope no one's dead!"

Rob

Oh no. Oh no. Oh no. Hands shake so bad, fumble my book. Can't shove it into my pack. Papers spill. Pen rolls away.

Drag my sorry self. Long hall. Floor designed to camouflage mud and puke. Dan coming from the other way. Open the office door. Sarah's already there.

Mr. White says, "Sit down."

Last time on this bench I'd sliced myself open on the table-saw in shop. Forty-seven stitches. This is worse.

Mr. White asks if we have anything to say.

I don't. Sarah doesn't.

Dan says, "Say about *what*? I don't know what you're talking about, man. Why'd you call me down here?"

Mr. White holds up our test papers. Mine's ragged. "Does this help jog your memory, Daniel?" he asks.

Dan still plays dumb. "Is that my test? What about it?"

Mr. White shakes his head. Says, "Anyone want to tell me how you got your hands on last year's exam?"

Dan says, "Huh?"

Sarah and I don't say squat.

All I can think is: My father's gonna kill me.

Mr. White gives the tests to the secretary. Tells us Principal Chen will deal with us. Leaves.

There are offices within offices. Mr. Chen's door is closed. I don't know if he's in there or not.

We wait.

Wait for him to declare our punishment. Order our execution.

If I could redo yesterday I'd ride down Hillhurst instead. Wouldn't see Sarah on her porch. Wouldn't swerve up her driveway. She wouldn't tell me about some kid giving her the midterm answer sheet. She wouldn't wave it in my face.

But at the time I felt like I won the lottery. Thought it was *my turn* for easy street. Had those answers in my pocket. Had Sarah Collier breaking rules with me. Felt like a million.

Idiot. Shoulda known it's *never* my turn for a break.

Too late now. It's all over. Unless I can talk Mr. Chen out of calling my house.

Tell him I'll stay after school for the rest of my life. Clean all the bathrooms, anything. Take fifty tests. Donate my organs. Just *please* don't tell my old man.

Jake

First of all, in my own defense, Sarah Collier is one of the most beautiful girls not just in this school, or city, but possibly in the universe. Not that I expect that makes a huge amount of difference, but picture this. No wait, first you have to know that I do not have a lot of what you'd call "friends" in school. Or, to be honest, out of school either.

And girls do not, as a rule, throw themselves at me. They more like throw themselves *away* from me. Or throw up at the sight of me. Anyway, you get the idea. So imagine how I felt when *Sarah Collier* plopped her books down on the table next to me at the library and flashed me her gorgeous toothpaste-ad smile.

It's true there were no other seats open, so it's not like she necessarily *chose* to sit next to me, but that didn't make me feel any less lucky. Like how you feel when a butterfly lands on you. Even though it's an accident, you take it personally.

Luck or fate or accident or whatever—I'd dreamed about

what I would do or say if Sarah Collier ever noticed I was alive. And now here she was, opening her books, digging in her purse for a pen. I offered her mine and she smiled at me *again*! That's *two* Sarah Collier smiles. And the next thing I knew, we were talking. Just a little. About school. About midterms . . .

How it got from borrowing a pen to my planning to loot my sister's room to supply Sarah with Beth's answers to the geography midterm, I do not know. And that's the truth.

How Sarah knew that I had a sister, or that said sister took geography with Mr. White last year, or furthermore that said sister was the type to keep and file old exams, I also do not know. Nor am I sure that she *did* know this. Maybe she said something about geography and I *offered* the rest.

Maybe I was mindlessly blabbing in an effort to make conversation. I don't remember. If it comes to a judge and jury, I'll plead temporary insanity. I'll throw myself on the mercy of the court. I'll . . .

But no one knows I was involved. That is, unless Sarah is selling me down the river. And really, why wouldn't she? No doubt she's telling Mr. Chen about me right now. Blaming me. Telling him I gave her the answers because I was trying to impress her. Claiming that I was trying to buy her affections. And of course, Chen and everyone else will believe her.

But it wasn't like that, at least not the way it sounds. I was just trying to help, just being nice. And if it comes to that, I'll tell Mr. Chen to take a good look at Sarah and put himself in my position. He was a guy himself once. And he's not blind. I'll ask him what he would have done if he were me. And he'll understand.

21

Sarah

Yesterday I was a hero. Today they think I'm scum. Well, la. That's how it goes.

Yesterday it was, "Oh heavenly Sarah! So generous and kind!" It was, "Oh sainted Sarah, who hath saved my scrawny rear!"

Now it's, "Sarah! You slime! Look what you made me do!"

See Dan. See Dan sulk.
See Dan convince himself
That I put a gun
To his empty head
And *made* him cheat.
See Dan's red face
Ready to kill someone,
Probably me.
Which figures.

Like they say:
"No good deed
Shall go unpunished."

It's my own fault. What was I thinking, sharing those answers with that worthless jock?

Rob hasn't blamed me yet, though. He just looks totally flipped, pale as a ghost, muttering that his old man's going to kill him.

And Jake? Yesterday he practically begged me to *let* him give me the answers. "Midterm's the same every year," he said. And I believed him.

"No problem," he said.
"Sneak into my big sister's room?
Snoop through her drawers?
Steal her answer sheet from last year?
Ride my bike to your house and hand deliver it?
No sweat," he said.
"Glad to help," he said.
"Happy to be of service!"

But that was yesterday.

He just now creepy-crept in here to the office on sticky bug feet, his eyes darting around. When he decided the coast was clear, he crept even closer.

"Please don't tell," he bug-squeaked. "Please, please, please, please. Don't tell on me."

Spineless cockroach.

As if I'd tattle. As if I'm a snitch looking to bring everyone down with me. As if that's *just* who I am.

Hey! Where's Katie? Her answers must've been wrong, too. Why isn't she here, sweating it out on this splintery bench?

Hmmmm. Could Katie be the one who tipped off Mr. Teacher?

Maybe Mr. White heard her clippity-clop-clippity-clopping over his bridge. Maybe he gnashed his evil troll teeth, and said he was going to eat her up for his evil troll dinner. Crush her bones to make his bread. *Fee fi fo fum*.

And she cried, "Oh no, Mr. Teacher-Troll! I'm just a short scrawny goat with dry stringy meat! Save your appetite for my big fat classmates:

"The delicious Daniel Goat Gruff! Yumm!

"The tasty Robert Goat Gruff! Double yumm!

"And the delectable Sarah Goat Gruff! Yumm yumm yumm!"

Would Katie do that? No way. Tell on us to save her own hide? No. I couldn't stand that. Not my Katie Potatie!

So where *is* she?

Mr. Principal's door swung open. He looked at me, curled his finger. "Ladies first," he said. "Sarah, will you step in here, please?"

Jake

I wish I hadn't done that. I shouldn't have gone down there and asked Sarah not to tell Chen about me. That wasn't very heroic.

If I were a nobler person, I suppose I would've dashed into the office and saved her. Maybe I would've told Chen that I'd tricked Sarah into using my sister's answers. A better man than I would have insisted that the entire cheating scam had been my idea . . . which, come to think of it, maybe it was.

I wish I hadn't crawled in there, low as a worm, on my belly. Now I'm cringing and wincing and I hate myself and I make myself sick. Feeling like mud is no worse than I deserve.

But it's not too late. I could go back down to the office right now. I could walk in there with my chin up, shoulders back, and I could save the damsel in distress.

It probably wouldn't make Sarah fall into my arms with gratitude, though. It would just make me the joke of the school.

"Jake Broder can't even *cheat* right! Can't even hide behind his genius sister without screwing up. Pathetic!"

And I *deserve* to be a laughingstock. For all I know, Sarah masterminded the whole thing. Stalked me. Followed me into the library and pretended to take the chair next to me by accident. I walked right into it like the biggest fool.

Who was I kidding? What were the chances, really, of a girl like *Sarah Collier* sitting next to me and flashing all those smiles at *me* for no reason? What are the odds that after never noticing me before she just *suddenly* gets so friendly out of nowhere?

I can't believe what a sucker I was, falling for the whole thing. I was duped. Tricked. Taken advantage of. Used. She must've been laughing at me the whole time.

And she never said anything about sharing my sister's test with other kids. Other *boys*. I thought this was just between us. I wouldn't have had any part in it if I'd known she was going to spread it around. Especially to Dan and Rob, neither of whom would stop to piss on me if I was on fire.

I bet that's how she got caught: because of *them*. If she'd kept the answers to herself, she wouldn't be sitting in the principal's office right now. So, really, *Sarah* created this mess. And she has no one to blame but herself.

Dan

Chen's gonna ask how all this started. He's gonna ask how a guy like *me* got roped into such a stupid scheme. And what'll I say?

I'd ask Rob what his plan is, but look at him! Jeez. Someone oughta tell him to lighten up. Remind him that we'll laugh about this later.

I bet he'll throw himself at Chen's feet—beg for mercy. He thinks nothing Chen dishes out could compare with what his father could do.

And what about *my* father? Chen's probably going to call home, right? Aw, man, this is such a complete bummer!

Sarah's in there now, but the door's closed, so I dunno what she's telling him. I bet she's crying. Of course she is. "Boo-hoo, Mr. Big Strong Principal! Poor little me is sooooo, soooo sorry!"

It's no fair. When chicks cry, guys turn to mush and cave in. What do you wanna bet Sarah gets off scot-free?

And Rob'll tell Chen what a mean old cuss his dad is, then Chen'll take pity on his pimply hide and let *him* off the hook, too.

That'll leave just *me* to take the fall.

Chen'll make an example of me. Expel me. Announce it on the PA. Wouldn't he just love that? He's always had it in for me and the other guys on the team. I swear, the man hates sports. You can see him at the games. Everyone else is cheering their heads off, Chen's bored to tears.

Well, I'll tell him Sarah e-mailed the answers to me last night, which is the absolute truth. I'd asked her if she had the study sheet for the exam because she's in my class. And that's *all* I asked her for: the *study sheet*. But Sarah took it upon herself to send me last year's midterm answers!

And what was I supposed to do? Ignore them? Is there any kid alive who could just ignore the answers to a midterm when they're flashed onto his computer screen?

And if Chen asks me where Sarah got the answers, I'll say I don't know. Which is true. Last night, she said that all information was on a "need-to-know basis," in case any of us were captured and tortured as spies. I thought she was joking.

I bet Chen doesn't know it was Sarah who started all this. She's probably in there right now looking like she looks, crying and telling Chen that she's totally innocent. Man! I bet she's blaming the whole thing on me!

Rob

Gotta explain about my dad. Quick, before anyone answers
the phone. Gotta hurry, make Mr. Chen hang up and stop
trying my house . . .

So why can't I speak?

Ruby

Okay, so my girls Ashley and Brenda come tearing into the lunch room, like, begging me to tell them why Danny was called to the office.

And I'm all, like, "How should I know?" I'd heard his name called over the speaker. Me and the rest of the school—we *all* heard his name *and* Sarah's! And Rob's, too.

Bren says, "Come on, Ruby. We don't keep secrets from *you*!" And Ash goes, "If Danny? Gets like suspended or something? They'll kick him off the team."

And I'm all, like, "Ask me if I care." But so much for cool—next thing, my mascara is black-bleeding stripes through my blusher and my girls are hugging me, and I tell all.

Then Ashley says, "I absolutely? Like totally do *not*? Believe? Even for, like, a second? That Danny? Like, you know? Dumped you?"

And Brenda's all agreeing. They both figure there's been, like, a *misunderstanding* or something. They think me and

Danny are totally like the greatest couple and so perfect for each other and in love and all that. So I begin to wonder if they're right and maybe I'm being unfair. Then, for like two and a half seconds, I feel bad for poor Danny, in the principal's office.

But please. He's there with *Sarah*! They're in trouble *together*.

Ask me if . . . oh, never mind.

Dan

Sarah came out of Chen's office, but I didn't get a chance to really look at her because he called me in right away. The first thing he asked was how I got ahold of last year's test, and I told him I got it over the Internet. Which is true.

Then Chen called my mom. I could tell from his end of the conversation that she was in the car on her way somewhere and was *not* happy about being derailed like this.

Chen's voice got tight as he said, "No, Mrs. Brand, this cannot wait until after your appointment. Your son Daniel is in my office *now*."

After that, Chen sent me back to the bench and called Rob in. Once the door was closed, I asked Sarah if she had told Chen who she got the test from, and she said, "No!" As in, *Of course not!* So she probably got the test from some girlfriend of hers, like Katie or something. You know how chicks all stick together.

Or maybe some *guy* gave her the test. Some dude that she's really got a thing for. Someone she's protecting. Man, the lucky dog! If I'd known you could get a chick like *Sarah Collier* in exchange for a *test*, I woulda gotten a few tests for her myself!

Ruby

After lunch I, like, ditch Ash and Bren and tiptoe by the office. Through the glass I can see Sarah and Rob on the bench next to Mister You-know-who himself. His foot's twitching like it does before a game. He doesn't see me. None of them do.

Ms. Gold, the secretary, is fiddling around with paper on the counter, so I can't just, like, waltz in. I pretend to read the announcements on the board outside the door. There's still an index card up for Mrs. Kaliman's free kittens, who are probably, like, grandparent cats by now. And I'm all, like, How long can a girl stare at ancient notes on a message board?

So I knock on the glass, and *finally* Danny looks up.

I roll my eyes, like, *You doofus. Now look what you've done!* And I smile, like it's all a big joke. And he smiles back, all cocky.

Sarah half-smiles, too. And not the kind of smile you'd give a girl whose boyfriend you just stole. So who knows?

After an eternity Ms. Gold comes out, so I catch the office door and stick my head in.

Danny whispers that Chen is calling their *parents* and that they don't know if they're, like, *suspended* or not. He sounds practically *proud* of himself.

Not Rob, though. His neck is hanging and his head's, like, dragging on the floor. He looks up for a second and gives me this totally scared-rabbit look.

So I'm all, "But what did you guys, like, *do*?"

Rob moans and drops his head. Sarah sighs and looks totally embarrassed.

But Dan-the-man looks *exactly* like his usual smug self. He goes, "We didn't do nothin'!" Then a little quieter he says, "White and Chen think maybe some of our answers weren't strictly *legit*." And he, like, *winks*.

Then the principal's office door opens, so I scoot.

Now I'm thinking: Answers not legitimate? Meaning??? That he, like, *cheated* or something? He got busted for cheating on his midterm?

Is *that* what he was talking about this morning? Ick! How gross is that? And it must've been something *much* more grand and glorious than just sneaking a peek at someone's paper if it included Rob and Sarah, and got them *all* benched like that. And, like, broadcast on the PA no less!

"ATTENTION, EVERYONE! ANNOUNCEMENT! Ruby's boyfriend is so totally stupid that he has to cheat to pass his stinking midterm!"

Eew! That makes *me* look like trash that hangs with, like, lazy misfit losers. Eew! Eew! Eew!

I could die. I hate him. I totally hate his stupid guts. *Danny, I hate you!!*

35

Dan

Mom marched in so mad that sparks flew. First she lit into Chen, asking if he realized what a remarkable person I am. "Daniel's well thought of by his peers," she said. "Indispensable to his team. Excellent grade-point average. Involved in several extracurricular activities. Studying pre-law."

Law? That was news to me. I been thinking TV, a sportscaster maybe. But you could tell that Chen was starting to sweat.

Then Mom demanded to know what *proof* Chen had that I was involved in this mess. So Chen showed her our three test papers. Rob's looked like he used it to clean the mud off his boots, but you could still tell we all had the same answers.

Without missing a beat, Mom changed her battle plan. "Do you have any idea how much money I've *personally* raised for those new auditorium seats, Kevin?" That was a good touch, using his first name like that. But she might have overdone it when she added, "You'd think, *Kevin*, that the

36

hundreds of volunteer hours I've put in for this school would count for something!"

Chen mumbled that her involvement was appreciated but irrelevant.

Mom continued through clenched teeth, saying that he better think twice before he puts this on my permanent record or gets me booted off the team. "This could destroy my son's chances of getting into a top school," she said. "You could ruin his entire future!"

"I didn't do this to him," Chen said. "Daniel did this to himself."

Then he lectured all of us for a while on how bad it is to buy and sell tests, that the value of a true education is not in the grades, and on and on. While he was ranting, I was thinking, Hey, man, that's not a bad idea! A guy could really clean up around here selling grades! Of course, one screw-up like this—wrong test, failing mark—could cost you everything.

Then I noticed that Chen was telling us we're *suspended*! All of us—me, Sarah, and Rob—until he finds out how we got last year's test.

I protested, saying, "That's not fair! Why should *I* be suspended? I don't have a clue where Sarah got the stupid test! Ask *her*!"

Rob kicked me in my shin. *Ouch!* But if he wants to be a hero, that's his business. They can leave me out of that noise!

Chen looked at Sarah.

She shrugged, calm, cool, no tears. "Dan's right," she said with a sigh. And I coulda kissed her.

So Chen lessened my and Rob's punishment. Now we're

just on probation, meaning the least little screw-up and we'll be off the team. And he told us we have to write some essay thing about cheating. And then it was over. Not so bad, really. We even got the rest of the day off.

Mom hoofed it out of there and I was on her tail. But when we got to the car, she went nuts and started shrieking at *me*! Man, she was loud enough for the entire school to hear. I ducked low in the passenger seat, saying, "Yeah, well, could you start the car, please? Could we maybe talk about this at home?"

But no. We sat right there while she launched into a list of things I can never do again. An *extreme* list, I might add. Such as watch TV, listen to music, play Nintendo, breathe, or blow my nose. Then a list of chores I'm going to have to do: carry out the trash, clean the garage, vacuum.

Then she started in on how ashamed she was, and disappointed in me, blah, blah. I never got a chance to say a word.

As she finally started the car and we headed out of the parking lot, she told me, "You can just forget about going any- where, and I mean *anywhere*, for the next . . . well, I haven't decided how long. Your father and I will have to discuss your punishment, but I assure you, young man, you can expect to be grounded for a good long time."

I slid further down in the passenger seat to glare out the window, thinking, Great, man, just great. Ruby's gonna go ballistic if I miss her sister's shindig.

Sarah

When Lilly (my mother's assistant) told my mother that the principal was on the phone, Mom instantaneously freaked, thinking there'd been a disaster, an earthquake, a shooting. She said she pictured spattered blood, me dying, crying out for her. So when Mr. Principal told her that I'd been caught in a cheating ring, my mother was relieved. She cheerfully told him she'd be right there.

But in the car, said my mother, she started thinking about cheating, and she got so depressed that by the time she got to school, she was practically in tears, imagining herself as an eighth grader (like me), and thinking about how little faith she'd have to have in her own abilities, and how low her self-esteem would have to be, to make her cheat. (She "shared" all this with me on the drive home.)

There was no point in telling her that my getting in trouble was not about *her* as an eighth grader—because in my mother's mind *everything* is about her. So as she drove, I sat back and dutifully listened to her lengthy monologue about how times have changed. How she recognizes that the pressures to succeed are much tougher for my generation than they were for hers.

And that the newly blurred line
between right ——— and wrong
must ———————————
——— be ———————
——————————— hard
to ———————————
——————— navigate. ———

But mostly my mother discussed how difficult it is

to be

a responsible

single

parent

in these,

quote,

morally

ambiguous,

unquote,

times.

Of course she didn't forget to add that it wasn't *her* fault that she was a single parent. She'd been a perfect wife, and my father had been a perfect fool. The punch line to every one of my mother's lectures is basically the same:

EVERYTHING
is my father's fault
for leaving us.

But she can't just jump to that conclusion. She has to weave her sticky web of motives, fears, and psychobabble. My mother reads a lot of self-help books, and after eleven years of therapy she considers herself an expert. So by the time we reached our apartment she'd proclaimed that my cheating was because I blame myself for my parents' divorce. I don't think I'm worthy of my father's love. And I cheat in the pathetic heart-wrenching hope that if I get better grades, my father will love me more than he does his *new* daughter.

My mother had that all worked out, but when she came around to the part about my being suspended until I name the person I got the test from, she got quiet.

She said, "I can see that you're in a real bind. It's an ethical dilemma and we'll have to think hard about it."

In other words: She had *no* idea what I should *do* about the fix I'm in.

I promise you, though, that *after* I do whatever I end up doing, she'll have loads to say about why it was wrong,
> and all the
> deep,
> twisted,
> psychologically pathetic
> reasons
> that I did
> what I did.

Meanwhile, my mother said I should tell my father. She said that explaining the "event" to him would help me understand it myself, and that it would be part of my healing process. I think she was just afraid to tell him herself. Afraid he'd blame *her* for letting me get in trouble. He blamed her for my catching strep throat last summer!

Anyway, it ended with her crying and hugging me, and telling me she loves me, and promising to pay more attention to me and my *needs*.

Then she got on the phone to talk it over with her girlfriends, and I went to my room.

I knew I should call my father, but maybe it could wait till I saw him on Sunday. I was really in no hurry to hear what he'd have to say about it.

I checked my e-mail. The only message was from the boy who says he wants to lick the wax out of my ears. Is that gross or what? When I told Katie about him, she said she bets he's a man, not a boy. She thinks he's one of those perverted pedophile old guys who prey on innocent unsuspecting girls like me.

Maybe so, but sometimes he's funny.

I didn't write back. I didn't change my clothes or put on music or turn on the TV. I just wanted to sleep, even though it was only two-thirty in the afternoon.

Katie

My mum once told me that EVERYONE is hauling a load of putrid slop through life. Some of us have whole steaming backpacks full while others just have a stinky gob in their pocket—but everyone has SOME. So a year and a half ago, when my dad died, I figured: Well, here it is—my load to haul.

I knew its size (three or four suitcases full, at least). And I knew its stench (awful!). So I thought I just plain KNEW my load and that there wouldn't be any more surprises.

That was my first mistake: Assuming that having such a horrific thing happen to me meant I had ALL the load I was ever going to get. It seemed only fair that since I had a DEAD PARENT to deal with, I'd be spared the other nasty ordeals that kids have to face. I should be excused from atrocities like self-doubt, acne, shortness, insecurity, and flat-chestedness, right?

And shouldn't I be allowed to miss being falsely accused of tattling on my best friend?

It seems, no. My load just gets bigger and stinkier.

Here's what happened: I heard Sarah's name called over the PA system during second hour. Her name and Rob's and Dan's—all of whom are in my geography class. I was pretty sure I knew what it was about and I felt terrible. Well, to be honest, first I felt relief for MYSELF (that I hadn't used the answers), and THEN I felt bad for Sarah.

But I was trapped in my seat. And I had another midterm coming up in third hour, all the way across campus. So I couldn't go looking for Sarah between classes.

Then, during my algebra midterm, I happened to look out the window and saw Dan and his mum in the parking lot! Dan, as in called-to-the-office-Dan. Dan, as in Dan, Rob, and SARAH!

An orthodontist appointment? Slim chance.

So then I knew that the punishment for "Row, Row, Row Your Boat" was REALLY bad. They were being sent HOME! Poor Sarah!

When the bell rang, I threw my exam on my math teacher's desk and dashed to the office. Rob was there alone on the bench, looking shell-shocked. I felt sorry for him but I didn't stop to talk. He and I used to be really good friends, back when it wasn't so hairy and complicated to be friends with boys. Now, though, I was looking for Sarah.

I searched the halls until I finally caught sight of her and her mum heading out the door. I ran up to them, but Sarah barely slowed and she wouldn't even look in my direction.

"I am not going to ask why YOU weren't called down," Sarah said in the meanest little voice.

Huh? I was flabbergasted. I didn't want to go into it in

front of her mum, so I whispered, "I chickened out. I got scared and didn't use Animal, Animal."

Still not looking at me, Sarah, in a voice that was nothing but sarcastic, said, "I suppose Mr. Teacher noticed all by himself that THREE needle-thin tests out of the whole haystack of midterms had the same wrong answers? And he figured that out in less than TWO hours?"

"Well, duh, Sarah!" I said. "He MUST have!"

She finally faced me, but with a sneer, and added, "Isn't that AMAZING, Katie?"

Then her mum said, "Let's go, Sarah."

And they left me standing in the hall with my mouth open.

Rob

Temporary stay of execution. Mr. Chen can't find my parents.

Dan's mom comes. Tells Mr. Chen he has no right to be mean to her baby boy. Mr. Chen puffs out his mustache, glares through his bifocals. Can tell he thinks Dan's mom is a case. But keeps cool, doesn't raise his voice.

Mr. Chen thinks *we bought* last year's test answers. Says he doesn't want us seeking revenge on the person who sold us the test. Wants to handle it his own self. Fine by me.

Never occurred to me that whoever gave Sarah the test coulda fed her the wrong one *on purpose*. That reeks. Can see the temptation to pulverize the creep who'd do that to her.

Mr. Chen asks *again* how we came to possess the test. Threatens to suspend us. And Dan rats Sarah out without a flinch. "Ask *her*!" he says, pointing. "*She* gave me the test."

And Sarah doesn't miss a beat, says, "Dan's right. And I gave it to Rob, too."

Brave, confessing like that. I don't think I could've taken

the rap alone. She got me and Dan pretty much off the hook. We're suspended for today only. Mr. Chen tells us to write an essay about cheating, due Monday. And says there's no make-up midterm, the flunking test grade stands.

Sounds fine to me. Essay? Gladly write a novel. Flunking test grade? Fair enough. Just leave my parents out of this.

I don't say that, though. Don't say a thing.

Sarah's mom comes next. An older, twitchier Sarah. Maybe it's this scene making her jumpy, but she seems like the nervous type anyway. Looks ready to faint when Mr. Chen says that Sarah is suspended until she tells how she got last year's midterm.

"Maybe Sarah just needs a little time," her mom says.

Sarah gives her a look, grabs her stuff, and leaves. Her mom scurries to keep up. Mr. Chen goes back to his office.

I have the bench to myself.

I plan ways to explain about my dad's temper—nothing sounds right. Chen probably won't believe it anyway.

The minute hand lurches like it's barefoot on hot tar. If it makes it to 3:00 before Mr. Chen reaches my parents, I'll never cheat again, I swear.

But he calls me back into his cell at 2:48.

"Your essay on cheating is due Monday," he says.

"Sure thing, sir," I say. "No problem."

Then he writes "CHEATED" across the top of my exam paper. Red ink. Says, "I want you to explain to your parents what happened here today." Shakes the test at me. "Show this to them and have one or both of them sign on this line." He draws an ugly red gash across the bottom of the page.

"Return it to me first thing Monday morning."

Inside I go, *Yes!* I can forge their signatures, easy!

Vow to myself to be good as gold, a model student, ideal son, perfect upstanding American citizen for the rest of the year—the rest of my life.

But then he adds, "And have them call me Monday, or I'll be calling them. Got it, Robert?"

Crash.

I should plead, beg, cry. Do whatever it takes. But I say, "Yes, sir." Take the paper and leave.

Now what?

Ruby

Not that I *care*, but Danny isn't anywhere after school. Bren and Ashley are all, like, "You don't need him anyway. A guy like *that*." Meaning, I guess, a cheater.

I say nothing about how Brenda, like, constantly copies off me in history. But I guess that's different because she says she's, like, totally missing the brain cells that can memorize, like, facts and numbers and all.

Not me. Not only do I remember the dates of all the, like, battles and treaties and wars and whatever in class, but I'm all, like, wall-to-wall memory. Want me to recite dates and times? I met Danny last year on, like, Tuesday, November 20, at 4:30 (maybe 4:45) p.m., in front of the library when Ashley and I were waiting for a ride home. And I can absolutely tell you that he, like, walked me home from school for the first time, on Monday, the seventh of January. It was drizzling.

Quiz me. When did he ask me to be his, you know, girl-friend?

January 14, at the rink.

When did he hold my hand for the very first time? (I feel like I'm gonna puke.) Or call me on the phone? Or wave to me from the ball field?

I've got all the, like, dates, times, places, and whatever, plus what I was wearing, what he was wearing, who else was there . . . all right here in my head.

Whether I like it or not.

Rob

Bell rings. Classrooms bang open, kids explode out of everywhere. Bursting free, weekend.

No one touches me. Not bashed with a shoulder, rammed by a backpack, elbowed. Invisible shield.

Start to trudge home, slow heavy legs. But don't turn right on Denver. Keep straight.

Past the park.

Mall after mall.

An overpass way out there.

It gets dark. No plan, just following my feet. Due north, one foot, the other.

Ma will be worried. Should stop, call home. Intend to, in a minute. At the next phone booth, or the one after that.

Notice the perfection of the half-moon.

Backpack gets heavy. Dig in all the pockets looking for something to eat. Find gum. Ditch the rest of the pack behind a bush. Keep walking.

Concentrating on my thoughts. Hypnotized blank by the slap, slap of soles on sidewalk. Stumble across a street. Cars screech, honk.

Wouldn't be all bad if their brakes fail. If one hits me, would take care of everything, for good.

Katie

I couldn't believe Sarah thought I'd betrayed her. HOW could she think that? I consider her my very closest friend. It's true that our relationship isn't all cookies and cream, but I've always thought we were pretty close. Wrong AGAIN?

After Sarah and her mum left me, I wandered the halls feeling b–a–d. A) HURT that Sarah could think so little of me. B) SCARED that she might not get over it and our friendship would be finished, kaput, the end. Then C) MAD for being wrongly accused.

Hurt, scared, mad, hurt, scared, mad. Around and around in dreadful little circles like a snake choking on its tail. YEECH!

Plus, fourth hour had started, and I didn't have an excuse or a hall pass.

I peeked into Ms. Divan's office. Ever since my dad passed away, she had been more like a friend than just a guidance counselor. But there was someone else in her office. All I could see was the back of the other girl's head, so I don't know who it was.

A little clump of jealousy stuck in my throat, but I swallowed it down, reminding myself that A) Ms. Divan is SUPPOSED to be nice to other kids besides me, that's her JOB! And B) What would I have told her anyway? That I'd been planning to cheat but chickened out? That I felt guilty for NOT cheating???

Ms. Divan looked at me over the other girl's head. She gave me a tiny smile and tilted her head in a way that meant, "Come back later." But I knew I wouldn't.

I slipped into class, trying to look pinkish—hoping Mr. Bowers would think I had some unmentionable bathroom-related reason for being tardy. Then I spent the rest of the hour slumped in a lump, wondering if Sarah really, REALLY thought I had turned her in.

Here's what I told myself: Sarah's just upset, and who wouldn't be? Getting dragged to the office. Having her mum called. She'll come to her senses and realize I had NOTHING to do with her getting in trouble. Sarah has a quick temper but she doesn't STAY mad, and I was sure she'd be over it by the time I got home. At least I hoped I was sure.

The whole rest of the school day and all the way through orchestra rehearsal, I tried to plan what I'd say to her. I'd call her when I got home and say . . .

Actually, SARAH should call ME! She should call and BEG me to forgive her—for accusing me. For not trusting me. For insulting me like that!

But in case she didn't, what could I say? I'm sorry I didn't cheat? I'm sorry you think I'm the kind of friend who'd tattle?

Meanwhile, Ms. Bazikian pointed her baton at me TWICE. I hate that.

Then the kid who shares my music stand said, "Bummer about your friend Sarah." She probably meant to sound sympathetic, but it only made me screech my violin even worse. Ms. Bazikian stopped the entire orchestra and made everyone wait for me to retune. Talk about EMBARRASSING.

Dan

When my dad came home, Mom got hysterical all over again. She was going on about how she won't be able to show her face anywhere. And she was especially ticked because the PTA something-or-other was coming up and she's one of the co-chairs. "How will that look with everyone knowing?" Her voice was so high and sharp that I checked my ears for blood.

Then Dad said, "Hey, calm down. Don't make a federal case out of this. It's nothing. Just forget it." He said, "Everyone cheats, Marcie, honey. Read the newspaper, look around you. I bet you can't point to *one* businessman who doesn't bend the rules from time to time. Name a politician, a priest for God's sake! A president!"

"But . . ." Mom said.

"But nothing," Dad replied. "I think that Chen fellow over-reacted."

Mom continued to whimper, but less.

"I'm sure this whole thing'll be forgotten by Monday if it

56

isn't already. But listen, honey, if it comes down to it, I'll have a few words with Brian Matthews."

Mom said, "Who?" and I was glad, because I didn't know the name either.

"Brian Matthews? The superintendent of the whole dang school board? We golf together, you know."

I shouldn't have laughed.

Dad looked up and saw me in the doorway. "What are you snickering at, joker? Think this is funny?"

I could've kicked myself.

"You think I'm *proud* to have my son caught cheating? Do you think I'm *pleased* that you got your mother dragged into school to hang her head in front of your principal?"

I shook my head, still hoping to get some of the punishment lifted.

"No is right," he said. "I am *not* proud. Not one bit."

Mom was nodding her head off, like, "Go get 'em!" She said, "I told him no more Nintendo, TV, or music, and he's grounded. And from now on he has to help with—"

Dad raised his hands as if to protect himself from her bullets and said, "Whoa, honey! Let's not get carried away! He's just a kid. And it's not like he *killed* anyone." He chuckled, and I knew everything was cool.

I wanted to chuckle myself, but I didn't.

Dad said, "He just made a bad judgment call. Right, son?"

"Right, Pop!" I answered.

Mom tried to object, but when she started to sputter, Dad put his arms around her. "Aw, honey, I know you're upset," he said, winking at me behind her back. "But boys will be boys."

Ruby

Okay, so Mom calls me to the phone. *"It's Dan!"* she says, like I should be all thrilled to, like, death.

I glare at her to say I'm not, like, home. But she totally ignores me and just clunks the phone down on the table.

I glare again, but what's the point? So okay, I lift it like it's a dead rat, and totally bored I'm all, "Yeah?"

And Danny goes, "Ruby? That you? What's the matter?" All Mr. Sweet.

And I'm like, "Don't give me that." And go, "Maybe *Sarah Collier* likes cheats, but not everyone does."

And he starts to, I don't know, tell me he's sorry? And says he doesn't like Sarah *that way* or whatever.

So I go, "Yeah, sure."

And he goes, "I'll be right there and we'll talk about it face-to-face."

And I'm all, "What makes you think I'd *want* to talk to you face-to-face?"

Then he, like, has the nerve to say something about it being *my fault* that he cheated!

That blows me away. And I'm, like, totally, *"Excuse me?"*

So he says that I kept him so busy helping set up my sister's party that he never got a chance to study.

Yeah. Right.

Okay, so that's when I, like, say something that I can't repeat, and I, like, hang up. On him.

Meanwhile, my mom and my sister are, like, *shrieking* at each other for a change. They've been at it pretty much nonstop for weeks, and it's like, Okay, I get it. When it's my turn, I'll elope.

But elope with who?

My mom *l-o-v-e-s* Danny. My dad, too. Even my sister says he's a "stud-muffin." Well, they can have him. They can just, like, chop him in thirds and share him. Ask me if I care.

So how come all these tears keep, like, streaming out of my *face*???

Dan

Man, can you believe that chick? Typical.

As long as I'm cool and everything's rosy, she's fine. But the second the chips are down—is she sympathetic? Understanding? How about even *civil*? Isn't a girlfriend supposed to be loyal and stand by you through thick and thin and all that?

Gimme a break. I don't need this noise.

I'm just glad she let her true self show so I don't waste one more second on her.

I never really thought Ruby was so hot anyway. If you want to know the truth, I don't know why I stayed with her for all these months. Habit? Laziness?

I'm *glad* it's over.

And now I can skip that stupid engagement party thing tomorrow. Cool! I was dreading it. Gives me the creeps having her and her whole clan looking at me and licking their chops, like, Oh boy, maybe we can hook this one next!

Phew! That was a narrow escape.

I wonder if Sarah got in trouble today. Her mom seemed pretty calm at school. Of course, a full-blown *hysteric* would seem cool compared to *my* mother.

Maybe I'll give Sarah a call and see how she's doing. We're in this together, after all.

Sarah

I woke from a nightmare and stumbled to the bathroom around midnight. On the way back to my room I saw my mother sitting perfectly still in the den, holding an empty wineglass.

"You okay?" I asked.

I startled her. She jumped a little. Then she said, "I was thinking about *cheating*. It's such a loaded word. Cowboys in the movies shoot each other dead for cheating at cards," she said. "When I found out that your father was cheating on me,

I

wanted

to

die."

Here we go, I thought. Time for the what-your-father-did-to-me talk. Oh goody! Now the two of us could commiserate like two old crones, about Father's betrayal of Mother and Katie's betrayal of me.

But this time my mother didn't go on about the divorce. Instead she said, "Maybe I shouldn't tell you this, but I cheated on a science test when I was in sixth grade. I completely forgot about that until tonight. We were studying the human body."

(I almost hooted, picturing *my mother* in sixth grade.)

"I remember sitting at the kitchen table," she said, "carefully writing the names of the bones and the nerve groups on the cover of my blue binder." Mother raised her glass to her mouth, then remembered it was empty and put it back down.

"My plan was to accidentally-on-purpose leave my binder where I could see it during the test," she explained.

I did *not* mention that I'd done that myself a few times. But (tee-hee!) imagine my mother being so daring back then!

Then she said, "I hardly slept that night, worrying about getting caught. I changed my mind with each toss and turn from bedtime till morning, excited, terrified. But it didn't occur to me that I could use all that intense energy to just study."

I hoped she wasn't going to ask me if I'd tortured myself like that last night, because I'd slept like a lamb. She didn't ask.

So then I figured she was going to tell me that at the last moment she pulled a Katie—

　　　　too much moral fiber,

strength of character,
or goody-goodyness
to be able to pull off such a ghastly crime in the light of day.
But no, my mother said that in spite of her
clammy hands
and shaky knees
and cotton mouth,
she *did* end up cheating off her binder, and she got an A. She said it was the best mark in the whole class and her parents were proud as Punch.

I was afraid the preach part was coming *now*—the garbage about how guilty she felt accepting their praise. Or how her success tasted like ashes in her mouth. But my mother even spared me all that!

Instead she said, "I'm trying to remember *why* I did it. All I remember is how hard my heart hammered, pretending to drop my pencil, then scratching an imaginary itch on my ankle so I could sneak a peek at my binder. My *blue* binder— I even remember the exact shade. And I remember that the terror of getting caught made me sick to my stomach. Now I wonder why it was worth it to me."

"You wanted to get a good grade?" I yawned.

"I doubt it was that simple," she said, insulted.

Her own past fascinated her, and she thought I should be deeply interested, too—even in the middle of the night.

You'll notice she didn't ask *me* why *I'd* cheated. But if she had, what would I have said?

Well, I wouldn't have *said* anything. But what was the truth? The secret truth? Was there one?

<u>Why not?</u>

He offered ——————————I accepted.
It was as simple ——————— as that.
If he'd offered me ——— a stick of gum
I would have accepted that ——— instead.

And it saved me hours of studying (or I *thought* it would). And who did it hurt?

My father cheating on my mother hurt *her*. Badly. Not just *hurt* her, but more or less wrecked her life. Look at her now, all mangled and achy, and it's been years.

Five, to be exact.

And when cowboys cheat at poker, they get the other cowboys' money. But who gets hurt when someone cheats on a test?

Well, if I was getting brain surgery, I'd like to be sure my surgeon didn't cheat his way through medical school—didn't buy a passing grade in "How to open, repair, and close the human head."

But mine was a geography test, so who did *my* cheating hurt? Or, rather, who would my cheating have hurt if I'd gotten away with it? If Mr. Teacher hadn't changed the midterm from last year, if the answers had been right and I'd gotten an A. It wouldn't have hurt the kids who studied for their A's. They'd *still* get them. And—

"Sarah! You haven't been listening to a word I've said!" my mother barked. "That's so rude! So disrespectful! Have you any idea how hurtful it is to be tuned out like that?"

"Sorry," I said. "I'm really tired."

65

"Well, go to bed then," she answered, still pouting.

So I did.

But I couldn't sleep.

And I didn't feel like reading.

I got out of bed and checked my e-mail. I knew there'd be a message from Katie, and there was.

It said:

S,

I'd NEVER do that and I can't believe you thought I would!

KT

To be honest, it wasn't just *hard* to imagine Katie ratting on me. It was impossible. But then again, like they tell us about prisoners of war and refugees—you never know how you or anyone else will act in a situation until you're in it. Not that this was the same, but . . .

I reread Katie's message, and I believed her. The relief of that belief (it even rhymes!) was delicious. But I didn't answer her.

There was a message from Dan, too, saying hi and asking if I was okay. I deleted him. Zap!

Then I sat looking at the keys, wondering what I could write for Mr. Principal's cheating essay that wouldn't be total drool. I'd like to write something honest. He hadn't said how long it had to be or anything. Maybe I could just say:

Cheating is confusing,
but getting caught is crystal clear.

Maybe I could turn it into a haiku!

I knew what he wanted and expected: a shamefaced apology, a claim that I'd been a wretched sinner but now I'm saved. That through the error of my ways, I'd learned my painful lesson and come to understand that "'Tis nobler to fail honestly than to succeed dishonestly,"

etc.

etc.

Spare me.

Rob

Moon is just a spot way out in space. Sitting on a curb in front of a piano store. Whole body vibrating. No idea how long I've been walking. Feels weird to stop. Soul keeps marching—doesn't notice it left its body behind. Can hear my pulse banging around in my ears, so I'm not dead.

Hungry, though. Sore feet and a stiff neck. Why *neck*?

Shoes off. Rub my heels. Feels so good that my soul comes rushing back to enjoy it. Take socks off. Toes have welded together. Pry them apart. Rotate head on my aching neck. Ahhh! Heaven.

But the motion knocks my brain into gear, makes me admit I've walked away. Haven't *run* away, but Ma will be just as worried. Dad will be furious. Hope he isn't taking it out on my little brother. Hate when he does that.

Wonder how late it is. Know I should call home. Slide into the doorway to rest first. Amazing how soft the cement is, how pillow-like the door. Dream about macaroni and cheese.

Saturday

Katie

It stunned me that there still wasn't an e-mail from Sarah in the morning. Imagine her sticking to the ridiculous idea that I'd told on her! One thing I THOUGHT I knew about Sarah was that she didn't stay mad for long. But, there I go again, thinking I KNOW something.

Maybe this WAS different. Maybe this time she wouldn't get over it. Wouldn't joke about it. Maybe she would just be done with me. Finished.

That would be so wrong! Not just because A) we'd shared practically every secret and thought for years and years. Or because B) she was my only good friend who'd known my dad alive. Or because C) I'd miss her so badly. But because D) I was being blamed for something I DIDN'T EVEN DO!

I staggered through the apartment as clumsy as a cartoon character who'd been bashed on the head with a frying pan.

Mum was talking on the phone and washing dishes. I could tell she was giving a client a pep talk. My mum is a dog trainer, and somehow the people who hire her think they can call any time they please to report that Fido piddled on their rug, dug up their hydrangeas, chewed their whatever, or bit the nephew. Mum always clucks sympathetically and reminds them to be firm.

She caught sight of me and waved a sudsy hand.

I waved back and poured myself some orange juice.

I heard her say, "Oh, can you hold the line for a quick sec while I get rid of this other call?"

She dried her hands on a towel. "Well, hi, Muriel," she said. Then she listened for a while, her face getting tighter and tighter until it looked ready to crack. At last she said, "Gee, I'll ask her," and turned to me.

"Katie," Mum said. "Do you have any idea where Rob is? This is Mrs. King on the phone. She says Robert didn't come home last night."

Mum's face was brittle as she waited for my answer. But for the longest time, I couldn't figure out something normal to say. Finally I yanked my jaw open and managed to squeak, "Rob?"

Mum nodded impatiently.

I cleared my throat, said, "Beats me," and managed what I hoped was a normal shrug.

My mum told Rob's mum that I was sorry but I had no idea where Robert might be. Then she wished Mrs. King luck tracking him down. I could tell Mum was trying to sound reassuring and calm. She said she was sure he'd turn up. Then she said something about teenage boys being naturally vexing, and laughed, ha-ha, as if Rob's disappearance was a childish prank. But her face was not amused. She asked Mrs. King to keep us posted. Then she hung up.

Mum flashed me a quick look, then clicked back to her dog client and apologized for the wait.

While she went on discussing carpet stains, I felt myself go cold. I suddenly knew Rob was DEAD. I could feel it down deep in my frozen bones, the same way I'd known that my dad was dead. The feeling was identical.

Suddenly Mum was off the phone and rushing over to grab my shoulders. "Why do you look like that?" she practically yelled, pushing her face right up to mine. "Tell me!"

Her eyes got wider, her voice higher. "KATIE, WHAT IS IT?" She rubbed my icy hands so hard it hurt and said, "BREATHE!"

Wasn't I breathing? I tried to inhale. Then I used every drop of air in my lungs to push out the words: "Rob's dead."

"Oh God! Oh God!" Mum wailed in a voice I remembered well. Then she was shaking me and asking question after question, fast, like arrows. "How do you know? Are you sure? What happened? Katherine, answer me! Oh God!"

The next thing I knew, the whole apartment was full of tears.

Jake

Any remaining grains of self-respect I may have had yesterday dissolved while I slept, and I woke up hating myself in the morning.

Not that self-loathing was entirely unfamiliar to me.

Countless mornings had begun with a similar sinking sensation: the recognition of myself in the flesh as compared to the person I am in my dreams. But today my gut sank even lower, knowing that my life as an invisible nerd was over—and my life as the kid most actively despised by the entire student body had begun.

My uncle Terry always tells me not to panic. He says that childhood and adolescence aren't for everyone, and that as long as I keep plowing forward, my life will eventually make sense. He claims that once I escape the small-worldness of middle school and high school—once I get to college—I'll find people more like myself. I'll recognize my species. I'll get happy.

Uncle Terry was a brilliant student as a kid, but he was picked on mercilessly for being geeky—and he got through it. And now he's a successful, well-respected man with a hot wife. He likes to tell me that a lot of the kids who picked on him in school got married right away and started having babies and getting fat and working dead-end jobs, and the best parts of their lives were over.

High school, Uncle Terry's low point, had been their highest high. He says it gives him untold joy to run into them now, all these years later. He is not above smirking.

I'm not a genius like him, and I've never really been tormented like he was either. I've mostly just been ignored. Until now, at least.

Now I cowered in bed half-expecting an angry mob of popular kids to burst in and drag me screaming from my room to avenge one of their own kind. I could picture all the thugs from the team armed with sports equipment, and Sarah's girlfriends wielding blow-dryers, singing the school fight song while ripping out my throat.

I had tons of studying to do, but I dug deeper under my blankets to postpone the coming day—to stall the rest of the weekend, the following week, the next months, the many years until graduation.

Katie

Eventually Mum and I calmed down and realized how silly we must have looked. Me, almost a grown woman, curled up in Mum's lap like a gigantic baby. Both of us on the kitchen floor, half under the table. The chair I'd been sitting on lying on its side. The kettle whistling its head off.

No, no, no, no. Of course Rob wasn't dead. No, I didn't have any idea where he was. I'd just thought . . . for that one minute . . . it had all reminded me of when the call came about Dad. It had been the same time of day. The same kitchen . . .

Slowly we got up, brushed ourselves off, and tried to act normal. We made toast and tea, and sat across from each other. But neither of us ate or drank.

"I wonder why Rob's mum called HERE," I said. Rob and I hadn't really been close in ages.

"She probably called everywhere she could think of," Mum said. "Poor woman must be terrified."

Then Mum asked if I had any idea why Rob would stay away all night. She asked me if he had a girlfriend.

I said, "Not that I know of."

"Does he do drugs?"

"Mum!"

"Well, does he?"

I said no, but to be honest I had no idea what Rob did these days. I hardly knew him anymore.

Rob and I used to be great friends. But one morning near the end of fifth grade I suddenly woke up with different eyes. My old pal Rob wasn't just Rob—he was a BOY. A cute boy. And the next thing I knew, I had a twelve-ton crush on him.

I could no longer breathe around him, let alone look him in the eye, talk to him, or act at all normal. I had uncontrollable giggling fits one minute and was furious at him the next. He'd say, "What's bugging you? You're acting weird!" And I'd be so offended, I'd burst into tears.

He'd ask me if I wanted to ride bikes and I'd drive myself batty trying to decide if that meant he liked me as a GIRL or thought of me as a BOY.

My feelings were hurt if he didn't notice things about my looks, even though in our whole lives he had never before said a SINGLE word about hair or clothes or anything like that.

I found myself always trying to figure out what he REALLY meant, as if he was suddenly speaking in code. But deep down I knew that I was the one who'd switched languages. It felt a lot like insanity. Or the way I imagine drugs would make me feel—exaggerated and out of control.

He kept saying, "What did I do? Why're you so mad at me

all the time?" And even THAT would upset me, because I thought that if he CARED, he'd be able to figure me out.

Well, he never did. He gave up on me instead, and our friendship was destroyed.

But that was years ago. NOW Mum was sitting here looking worried, not drinking her tea or eating her toast, wondering why Rob would disappear so mysteriously. I could tell that she was picturing him in trouble: abandoned in a ditch with two broken legs, or clonked on the head by bad guys, or the victim of a hit-and-run accident, lying unidentified in the hospital with amnesia . . .

I couldn't keep quiet any longer. I just felt too sneaky and greasy not telling her. First I swore her to secrecy, then I spilled the whole story, starting with A) Sarah giggling over the phone with me about a stray Santa's elf delivering midterm answers to her. And ending with Z) Sarah blaming me for tattling.

Mum gnawed on her knuckles while I talked. She does that when she's stressed.

Sarah

Katie didn't know I was over it, so when she called, she leapt
in speed-talking, thinking I'd hang up on her or something.
As if I'm a drudge to carry a grudge. Oh fudge.

> I'd never hang Katie
>   My captain, first matie
>   We won't separatie
>   Be pals till we're eighty
>   My Katie potatie.
>
>   Whatever debatie
>   No matter how weighty
>   Or how irritatey
>   I never could hatie
> My bestest friend Katie.

She (quickly) told me about Rob's mom calling, and about

Rob staying out all night.

"I know you blame me for this," Katie said. "But Sarah, you've gotta get over it! This is serious! And I'll say it one more time: *I did not tell Mr. White, Mr. Chen, or anyone else!*"

"Okay, all's forgiven," I teased—which was stupid, seeing as she didn't know I was over it.

"Who's asking for *forgiveness*?" Katie sputtered, exasperated. "I didn't do anything to forgive! Don't you get it?"

"All right, Katie," I said. "If it'll make you happy, then I *don't* forgive you. Better?"

Then Katie heard my jokey tone and got it that our fight was fought, our snit was snot.

"I'm sorry I was such a turd," I said.

She sighed, satisfied, and immediately changed the subject back to Rob's disappearance.

"Well, he was really flipped out over this," I told her. "He kept saying his dad was going to kill him. I suppose he could've really *meant* kill, as in shoot, stab, flay. As in ta-ta, so long, bye-bye."

Katie doubted it.

I went on, "And after Rob's dad killed him, he probably hid the body, and now he's pretending to act baffled. Using his wife's *genuine* bafflement as his cover!"

I laughed, and Katie practically bit my head off. She has *zero* sense of humor about death.

"You're right," I kept teasing. "They're probably both in it together. Mrs. King is playing the part of the worried, loving mother, wringing her hands, calling Rob's friends. Maybe hauling his photo to the police station. And His Excellency,

Mr. King, is no doubt pacing and chain-smoking as the frantic, heartsick, doting, desperately worried daddy-o."

Katie still wasn't laughing. I could tell through the phone that she wasn't even smiling. In a whisper she said, "Do you think Rob could have killed *himself*?"

I felt the hairs on the back of my neck jump to attention, but I said, "Rob? No way! He just . . . well, he just ran away, or he's staying with a friend or something. This is *not* a big deal."

Katie was still whispering. "Should we tell his parents about the test?" she asked.

"They already know," I said. "Mr. Principal called everyone."

But then I remembered that by the time I left with my mom, Mr. Chen still hadn't reached Rob's parents. "Oh, but wait," I said. "Actually, maybe they *don't* know. No one was home yesterday."

Katie

and

I

listened

to

each other

breathe.

"You're scared," she said.
"Am not," I said.
"Are too, I can *smell* it!"
"Through the phone?"
"You think Rob's dead!" Katie said, her voice shaking.

"Wrong," I answered.

"My mum thinks *we* ought to tell them."

"You said you didn't tell *anyone*!" I shrieked. "Your *mom* is anyone!"

"No, she's not," Katie said, giggling nervously.

"Well, are Mr. Principal and Mr. Teacher anyones? Some-ones? No ones?"

"Oh, don't start *that* again," Katie said. "Should we tell Rob's parents or not?"

"Not," I said. "I definitely vote *not*. It's none of our business."

"But—"

"If Rob wanted them to know, he would've gone home and told them," I insisted, although I wasn't nearly as sure as I pretended to be.

"Think positive," I said. "Think on the bright side: Maybe Rob was kidnapped and it's just a bizarre coincidence that it happened on the exact same day he got in trouble at school!"

"Why do I talk to you?" Katie asked. "It's like putting my mind in a blender." But then she finally laughed.

Dan

Rob didn't show up at practice and I wondered if his dad really *did* beat him senseless last night. Maybe he's in the hospital. Coach didn't say anything about anything, including about me being put on probation. Maybe he hadn't heard. In that case, I sure wasn't about to tell him.

After practice, I came home, scarfed down breakfast, and checked my e-mail. Sarah still hadn't messaged me back. That snob. Gets me into trouble, then just leaves me hanging? Forget her. I'd just been trying to be friendly.

Then in the shower, I realized that Ruby was probably getting ready for her sister's lunch thing. She'd made a big deal about how she wanted her dress to be a secret. Man, I bet she was going to look great.

I decided to surprise her. Get dressed up and just go over there in time for the party as if nothing had happened. I wished I'd bought some flowers or something, but my showing up ought to be enough. Ruby would be shocked, then happy. She'd probably give me a big hug and kiss—all forgiven.

So I got dressed, even put on regular shoes, and was heading out the door when my mom stepped in front of me and said, "Just where do you think you're going, mister?"

"What do you mean?" I asked.

"I mean, you can turn yourself right around, go back upstairs, and peel off your fancy duds," she said. "And feel free to wash off that half-gallon of cologne you're swimming in, too."

"I don't have time for this," I said, as patiently as humanly possible.

"Really?" said Mom. "My impression is that you have all the time in the world, what with being seriously grounded and all."

"*What?*"

"You heard me."

"Where's Dad?"

"Not here," she answered, and walked away as if the conversation was over.

"Hey, man!" I yelled. "I've *got* to go to Ruby's sister's engagement party. They're all expecting me! And I told them *weeks* ago that I'd be there for sure."

Mom didn't even turn around. "You should have thought of that *before* you cheated on your midterm," she said over her shoulder.

I stood dumbfounded in the doorway. Could she *do* that? Even though my dad had clearly lifted all that punishment off me?

Now I didn't know what to do. Go to the party anyway and deal with Mom later? She'd probably *doubly* ground me for ignoring her, and I didn't even have a guarantee that Ruby would let me in if I went over there. But if I didn't show up, that would *for sure* be the end with Ruby. She'd never get over it.

Jeez! Can you believe this whole mess? Remind me, in the future, *not* to let girls push me around.

Rob

Reach for a blanket. Hand fishing in empty darkness wakes me. Weird to find myself here, crunched in a doorway like an old wino. Hadn't noticed the cigarette butts and broken glass last night.

Get up and shake like a dog.

Have to whiz. No one's around, but still, even animals don't mess their nest. Go to the alley, take a leak on a Dumpster swarming with flies.

HUNGER!

Tough. No money. When'd I eat last? Must've been the cafeteria at lunch. Years ago. Can't remember what I had.

Rack my brain. Suddenly hugely important for me to remember my last meal. Like that would mean nothing has snapped. I haven't gone over the edge. It's perfectly all right to find myself here, having spent the night in a doorway.

Wring my brain like a sponge. Finally squeeze out a drop of memory: Had been too freaked about flunking the midterm to eat lunch. So last meal musta been breakfast before school yesterday. Too hungry now to do the work it would take to remember what that breakfast was.

Occurs to me there could be some semi–all right stuff in the trash. Not in this reeking Dumpster—but in some nicer garbage. Thought cracks me up: nice garbage.

Stand scratching, watching the sky get lighter at the edge. Ask myself, Now what?

Only answer: Keep walking.

But feet hurt bad from yesterday's blisters. Have to stop. Sit, then sprawl, on a bus bench. Catch a few more winks.

Wake in an entirely different world. Sunshine, traffic, stores open. Lady with groceries waiting for the bus four feet from my head.

Sit up. Feel scummy, stinky. Lady pretends not to notice me. I've done that: Tried not to stare at weirdos. Now *I'm* the weirdo.

Bus comes and the lady hurries on. Looks, no, *glares* at me through the bus window. Turns her head to stare longer until the bus carries her away. Must've thought I was a homeless drug addict loser, violent and crazy—sleeping on a bench.

Scratch my head. How long's it take to get fleas? My kid brother would think it was a riot if I got fleas. Hope he doesn't think I've left *him*. Hope Dad is leaving him alone. I should call.

Think of Ma, probably flipped out, imagining I'm lost or dead. Get up, look around for a pay phone. Find a broken one. Someone ripped off the receiver. I don't have money anyway.

Feet are killing bad. Starving, mouth tastes like a sewer. Find a working phone a few blocks down. Ask three different people for change to make a call. All three walk past like they don't see me.

Then notice the sticker right on the phone about collect calls. Raise the receiver, listen to the tone. Hope my kid brother answers. Ma is second best.

But what if Dad does? How will I explain worrying my ma like this? Have to tell him about the cheating stuff, too. Now he'll be ten times as mad that I've been cowardly, didn't come home and take my punishment like a man.

No winning this one. None.

Hang up. Sit down to think it through, plan my script.

A guy charges out of his store. "Shoo!" he yells, waving his arms as if I were a fly. "Move along, you! Just you keep moving."

So I do.

Ruby

I'm not looking what you'd call my, like, *personal best* today—last night's sob-fest left me all lumpy. But my sister has it worse: The star woke up with, like, a humongous screaming zit—right on her chin! No makeup in the world could hide that thing. I would've died.

Mom is wreck number two. Totally freaked over the table-cloths being, like, *peach* when the flowers are practically *apricot*, which is reason enough to slit your wrists if you're her. Then Dad gets an "emergency" call from some, like, client, and off he goes, swearing to be home in *plenty* of time for the luncheon.

Right.

As if we're new here. As if we don't know he's about to play "The Incredible Invisible Man!" Leaving Mom all smiling her head off, making excuses for him. Pretending his disappearing act is one of the quirky little things she just, like, adores about him.

Gag me.

Maybe Dad can't help it, or maybe he doesn't exactly, like, *kill* himself trying.

I'm all, "Mom, how can you stand it?" I'd put up with garbage like that from a husband of mine for exactly *not one second*. And that's a total promise. For sure. You can, like, *quote me*.

Anyway, it's all hopping downstairs. The kitchen's, like, totally crammed with caterer-ladies in tacky avocado-green aprons. Massive amounts of appetizers are being fussed over, arranged, heated. Our oven is probably in shock. It never even, like, *dreamed* of so much action in its entire life. And the whole place smells totally fattening.

One musician testing amps in the den is really cute and he, like, smiles at me.

Another guy is setting up a bar in the dining room.

More avocado aprons are setting the round tables. Mom is barking orders and looking totally insane.

I steal an apple and go out on the patio. Pretty, like, streamer thingies are looped around and there are flowers everywhere. It doesn't look or even feel like our house anymore. And the weather is per-fect-o.

Then I'm all, like, wondering what *my* engagement par-ty'll be like. And *bam*, I'm suddenly thinking of you-know-who and the whole mood is wrecked and I want to kill him. And if I cry one tear more I, like, *know* my eyes'll be two red blisters and totally gross out everyone at the luncheon. I start swallowing like mad and holding my eyes all wide open, so if there are, like, tears, they'll dry before spilling. Pathetic, no?

Then Mack, my sister's fiancé, shows up looking scared out of his wits. I guess about being, like, center stage in all this froth. It's hard to believe Mack is going to be my, like, brother-in-law. I've never had any kind of brother before. *In-law or out.*

I go, "My sister's upstairs using all the hot water—leaving exactly none for the rest of our showers." And Mack actually gets a little pink in the cheeks! Or maybe I'm hallucinating.

I'm, like, totally mute about her trying to melt her mega-zit, because I get the feeling Mack and my sister aren't the kind of friends, or lovers or whatever, who talk zits. Which is, like, seriously lame if you ask me, seeing as they're getting married. And how can anyone expect to keep pimples secret in, like, a one-bathroom apartment?

When *I* get married, I hope my husband and I will be so close that I'll be as comfortable squeezing *his* pimples as popping my own. Is that, like, too gross to be a romantic goal?

Anyway, I go, "I'll tell your *bride* that her *groom* awaits." And guess what Mack does. He absolutely, beyond a doubt, I swear on my life, *totally* blushes! Like, *red*!

I can't imagine *anything* on earth making Danny blush. That boy would moon the Pope without batting an eye. Name it, Danny would be game. That's exactly what I like *and* what I totally despise about him!

That's probably why he cheated. He probably gave it, like, zero thought. Just, "Free answers? Cool!" Would he for, like, half a second think about whether it was right or wrong? Forget about it. Not Bozo-the-Brave.

It makes him, like, fun and wacky. But who can trust a guy like that? A guy who lies on a test—a guy who thinks he's got, like, the *right* to an A that he didn't earn. You can never know what *else* he'll, like, feel comfy lying about. Or, like, how many girlfriends he'll feel entitled to at, like, the exact same time. Am I right?

How did we get back here?

I hate that. I started out talking about *Mack*, like, blushing or whatever—and blink! Next thing I knew, *Danny* had wiggled his sneaky self back into my, like, brain! That's *so* unfair!

It should be up to a person to decide what they're going to think about—and *when* they're going to think it. Otherwise it's like getting totally tricked by your own mind! Ooh, how sci-fi! How, like, out there!

I try to shake it out, like a muscle cramp, and I go upstairs. I'm all, like, yelling, "Groom downstairs!" into the steamed-up bathroom.

Then I go to my room and, like, *begin*.

I don't just "get dressed." Today I'm all extra super careful. From, like, curls to pedicure. A girl with a mission: I'm not leaving this room until I'm the absolute knockout million-dollar best I can be.

Part of me thinks Danny'll, like, show up on his knees, all begging me to forgive him. I don't know whether I will or not, but I sure want to look gorgeous while I take my sweet time and, like, *decide*.

Every time the phone rings, I expect Mom to go, "Ruby! It's Danny!" But she hasn't yet.

Never mind. The important thing is that I'm, like, having a good hair day and my dress is to die for and my soggy eyes are definitely looking more human as the morning goes on. Amen.

Sarah

Mother was at her yoga class, so I was home alone. I thought of writing a poem using only the letters in the word ALONE. One lone eon . . . but I didn't let myself. And I couldn't lie around listening to music either, because I had *three* midterms to study for.

Mr. Principal was having Dan, Rob, and me write essays on cheating. And as lame as that assignment sounded, it sure beat studying calculus. How about a research paper on: *Great Cheats in Fiction* or *Famous Historical Cheats*?

La. That sounded fun.

But the cheat paper was due Monday, and between then and now I also had to study for my other tests and do my regular homework, plus see my father tomorrow (unless he canceled on me again).

Nope, that wasn't exactly true. Nothing would be due Monday unless I told on Jake. No calculus midterm or any other test if I didn't turn him in. I'd just flunk? They'd *flunk* me for not tattling? How fair is that?

Well, I just couldn't believe Mr. Principal would really do that. I'd just go back to school Monday and act like nothing happened. And the bad, ugly meanness

would
all
just
blow
away
like
smoke.

I gathered the essential study tools and arranged them on the table in front of me: pistachios, pretzels, strawberries, grapes, carton of orange juice, drinking glass, shortbread cookies, dried pineapple. Then I opened my calculus book and spread out my worksheets.

I thought of calling Jake Broder and asking him if his sister took calculus last year (hee-hee). But I didn't think he'd appreciate the joke. I wondered if Jake was sweating it out this weekend, waiting for Mr. Principal to get word of his role in our little play.

How did it work, guilt-wise, I wondered. Was Jake as guilty as me? Was I more or less guilty than Dan and Rob? How much less guilty was Katie for not using the answers? Did that make her *entirely* innocent? Or did she at least get tiny black flecks on her soul for even *considering* cheating?

And how about if I *hadn't* got caught? Would that make

me guiltier or less guilty? Is there some kind of spiritual measuring stick or justice scales or something that assigns levels of guilt?

Hmm . . . there was a poem trapped in there, begging to get out. Calculus could wait.

Degrees of GUILT

1ST DEGREE
His first crime was stealing,
His next was revealing
His hot, stolen answers to me.
My crime was receiving
Those goods, then deceiving
My teacher with my treachery.

ADVANCED DEGREE
If guilt were a quilt made of patches
The icky green squares would be catches:
That's the unlucky few, who somebody knew
Were cheating in bits and in flashes.

The catches are caught and blamed.
Their parents are equally shamed.
Their faces turn red. They take to their bed.
But around them, life goes on the same.

96

Katie

I was practicing the violin piece that I'd messed up at rehearsal, when Mum knocked on my door. I pretended not to hear her. Sometimes that works, but not this time: She knocked again.

I hoped it would be something easy, short. When I let her in, I kept holding my violin and bow. But Mum sat down, then patted the bed for me to sit next to her.

"I don't know what took me so long to wonder this, Katie," she said, looking right at me. "But WHY did you cheat?"

"I DIDN'T cheat!" I said. "I TOLD you that!"

Mum said, "Yes, I know, but you INTENDED to. You memorized your Animal Animal song. I just want to understand why."

I shrugged. The truth was, I'd wondered the same thing. Sarah and I have always had secret alphabets and codes and clubs and crushes. And at first this cheat seemed like just another part of that. But telling Mum that I'd been doing it for FUN sounded so brainless.

And it was too pitiful to think (even in my own secret skull) that I was such a gutless wimp, I went along with the cheat plan just so Sarah wouldn't think I was a gutless wimp. I wanted Sarah to see that I was willing to take risks. When in fact I wasn't even willing to risk telling my best friend that I didn't want to take risks!

And Sarah wouldn't have thought less of me if I'd said no from the very start. She would've dropped the subject and not given it another thought. Right?

But that would have meant cutting myself out. I wouldn't have been part of it, and Sarah would have shared THAT set of giggles with other kids. It's humiliating to admit (even to myself) that I couldn't stand the idea of being left out of anything with Sarah. Yeech! If I didn't hate myself so badly, I'd pity me.

"No idea how you got into this?" Mum asked again. "None?"

She let that "None?" fester in the air between us awhile.

Then she asked what I'd decided to do about Rob's parents, as far as telling them about this whole situation—in case they didn't already know.

I HADN'T decided. I was getting a stomachache. I wanted to play violin.

Mum went on. "As a parent, I can tell you that if, God forbid, I were tearing my hair out over YOUR disappearance, I'd appreciate any information I could get my hands on."

I sighed.

Mum sighed.

I told her I'd think about it. Then I got up and lifted my

violin to my shoulder. She took the hint and left, closing my door behind her.

But I didn't play.

I called Sarah and asked her what she thought. But I could tell she wasn't listening. She said she was in the middle of writing a "cheating poem." That's so SARAH!

"But if you were Rob," I persisted, "would you think it was BAD or GOOD that I told your mum?"

"How should I know?" Sarah said. "Let your conscience be your guide, Katie Potatie." Then she hung up.

My conscience? I hunted around for it, in my brain. First I found: A) Pity for Rob's poor mum. And B) Pity for ROB for being afraid to tell his mean old dad. But then I found C) Maybe Rob's dad will get so scared by Rob's disappearance that it'll make him nicer when and if Rob comes home. (Actually, that was more about Rob's dad's conscience than MINE, right?)

I kept sorting through my brain until I found D), which was a snarky voice in there that said, "Butt out, Katie. This is none of your beeswax!"

Then THAT voice was drowned out by E), which said that if anything really horrible happened to Rob, it would be partly my fault for not letting his mum know what I knew. I'd hate to be one of those kids who don't take it seriously when their friends tell them things, then later wish they'd spoken up.

But ANOTHER inner voice—F)—reminded me that I only caught one quick look at Rob in the office. And I haven't really talked to him in ages. HE didn't tell me ANYTHING. So it's not at all the same as those kids who have to feel guilty forever, wondering if they could've changed history and saved a life.

And then there was G), that pesky, leftover-crush voice that I'd been trying to smother since fifth grade. The one that still suspected that Rob is my natural-born fate-mate, my destiny, determined by the stars.

How the heck was I supposed to know which one of those voices was my conscience? Why did everything have to be so COMPLICATED?

Rob

Watch a guy toss his burger scraps and drink in the garbage. Bright orange trash can, not beat-up and dirty. But people going in and out of the diner. Cars going by.

Go over and peer into the can. Almost whistle, casual the way a cartoon character would be. That makes me laugh out loud. Then, hearing myself laugh makes me feel like a crazy street person. Which, I guess, I am.

Feel all the strings cut loose—Pinocchio when he becomes a *real* boy. If I can reach in, pick out that man's leftovers, and eat them—I'll be a different person than the guy I was yesterday.

Already changed, but just on the surface—could still be reversed, washed off, undone. Once I've eaten out of a trash can, though, something *inside* will be changed forever.

A real boy. Me. The me who knows where the Rio de La Paz runs. No need for strings. No need to cheat. No need to fear.

Reach in, not with the cool of taking a snack from the

fridge, but not a guy sticking his paw into a nest of snakes either. Seems a long reach, like the trash can is getting deeper or the leftovers are shrinking back from my hand. Then fingers close around the cup—straw still poking through the plastic lid. Jolt of pure joy: It's half full and the ice hasn't melted.

Decide not to look—just discover by taste. Coke, Dr Pepper, Fanta, anything'll be okay. Take a long pull. Second jolt of happiness: It's lemonade. That's what I woulda ordered if I had the choice.

Yes!

I'm free. Shards of fear at my feet. They just *look* like broken glass.

Ruby

So the bass player's name is Ryan and he is really, really, I mean *really*, nice.

He asks me if I have, like, a boyfriend or something, and I go, "I did until yesterday when he was caught cheating."

And Ryan's all, "Guy's out of his bean to cheat on a girl like you."

So I crack up and go, like, "Not *that* kind of cheating! He cheated on a midterm—like, in school!"

I can tell that Ryan doesn't absolutely for sure see why a person has to, like, break up with another person for cheating on a test. But then he thinks about it for a while and he goes, "Wow! You're strict!" Like he *likes* that!

And I'm all, "Cheating is gross. And it was, like, geology or geography or something—not worth *taking*, let alone totally not worth getting in *trouble* over, or whatever. Plus, how can you, like, *trust* a cheater?"

Anyway, I don't mind Ryan thinking I'm all, like, super-honest or anything.

He's really good on bass. I mean *way* good.

And there are hordes of other boys here who are paying me, like, all kinds of attention. Older guys. My brother-in-law-to-be's friends. I'm dancing with absolutely, like, *everyone*. So ask me if I miss Danny for even one tiny second.

The answer: Danny who?

Rob

No roadblock, cliff, wild river without a bridge. Nothin' to stop me from moving on. I'm just ready to stop.

I turn around, head back, knowing I'm the guy who knows where the Rio de la Paz is because I'm the guy who lives my life. Good or bad, I'm the guy who has my old man as a father. Getting the Rio de la Paz answer wrong would have been like erasing myself.

Don't know what time I walked till last night, or what time I woke and started this morning. Figure it took about eleven hours to get here. It'll take longer getting back— messed-up feet, hungry, thirsty. It's hotter out.

Walking toward life. Home, school, all that. Heading back. Hours to plan what I'll tell my dad.

Or so I thought.

Police car veers up. Two beefy blue uniforms come at me. Arms bowed, ready to draw.

"Hey, buddy," officer says, "you wanna tell us why you're staggering like that? Where're you supposed to be?"

Put my hands up in surrender. Don't shoot!

Wouldn't it figure? Blam! Blam! Game over. Now that I'm ready to play?

Sarah

Punishment Poem

'Tis a lie to pretend that I read the text.
'Tis a lie as well for which I'm hexed.
For I do NOT know the sea from land,
I'd still be lost with map in hand.
For I did not cram
For this exam.
You bet I regret not doing the work,
And now I feel like a total jerk.
But that's not punishment enough!
It must be meaner! Must be rough!
Unless I rat, I'll have to roast.
Tattle or I'm freaking toast!
But though you burn me as a witch,
You gots to know: I ain't no snitch!

Rob

Imagining neighbors peeking through curtains. Muriel and Mike's son Rob, brought home in a squad car.

"I knew *that one* would come to no good," Mrs. Whatsername on the corner'll say.

"Yup," the shriveled one agrees. "Always was a bad seed. Broke my window with a baseball, *twice!*"

Poor Ma. She'll hate this.

Pull up behind a strange car in the driveway. Whose? People on the porch. Katie? Katie and her mom? Selling Girl Scout cookies? Nah, that was years ago.

Ma pushes past them, racing down the walk, arms out. Cops open the door for me—mine has no inside handles.

Ma hugs me, crying. When did she get so short?

Over her head I see Dad come out the screen door. Katie and her mom slip into the neighbors' yard.

My father doesn't come any closer.

Ma invites the officers in for cake. They say no, thanks. Get back in their car, drive quietly away. Only voices left are sparrows in the roof tile.

Ma takes my arm. We go up the walk.

I clear my throat. "Why was Katie here?"

Ma whispers, "She told us."

"About the test?" I ask. "She told *both* of you?"

Ma nods.

"She told you I got in trouble?" I ask to be sure.

Ma pats my arm. "We're just glad you're home and all right."

The expression on my father's face is unreadable. Doesn't move or speak. We walk past him into the house. *He* seems smaller too. Shorter.

Straight to the bathroom. Lock the door. Hot water feels great. Best shower of my life.

Go to my room, lock the door, fall on my bed. Don't care that my feet stick out in space. Don't care about nothing.

Little brother knocks just as I'm falling.

I grunt.

"Robby? You okay?" he asks through the door.

Say, "Yep, just tired."

"Sure?" he asks.

I say "Yeah" with my last ounce of strength. Then sleep.

Katie

Maybe Mum was right. Rob's parents did seem relieved that there was a REASON he was missing and it wasn't that he'd been mysteriously abducted by aliens or kidnapped by bandits.

But can you imagine how stupid I felt when the police car pulled up, and there I was? Rob probably thinks I'm a nosy, gossiping sticky-beak.

Yeech! I just wanted to evaporate, but Mum and I couldn't LEAVE because the police car was blocking the driveway! We hid around the side of the house. My cheeks burn just thinking about it.

Anyway, when we finally got out of there, Mum was either A) sorry she'd made me go, or else B) it was her way of thanking me. But in any case, we stopped at the mall and she bought me those expensive jogging shoes I've been drooling over. They're really cute. I'm going to wear them to school Monday.

I wonder if Rob's going to be there.

Sarah said she's not supposed to go to school until she tells the principal WHO gave her the test. But she's going to show up Monday and just act normal. She thinks that once Mr. Chen has had a chance to cool down, he'll forget the whole thing. I hope so.

I thought it sounded scary either way. To go to school or not to go. To tell or not to tell: THAT IS THE QUESTION.

For once, I'm glad I'm not in Sarah's shoes.

Sunday

Sarah

My father was *two and a half* hours late, but at least he didn't cancel. He said something about a big case for a finicky client (Dad's a lawyer). I don't remember the details, but
of course
it was through
no fault
of his own
that he was late.

Thankfully, he showed up alone. Not that my half sister isn't adorable, but still, it's nice sometimes not to have to watch her eat with her hands.

At Sunday brunch, the Overland Cafe is always full of divorced dads and kids on best behavior. So first we had to wait in line. Then we had to wait to order. There was plenty of time to study the menu, although I'd memorized it years ago. My father probably had, too—not that it mattered, since he always orders the same thing:

Two poached eggs
A plain bagel—dry
A small grapefruit juice
And a decaf-lowfat-double-latte.

His diet is thanks to Maria, his (new) wife, who he says is keeping him young and happy—implying that my mom was the wife who made him old and miserable. Which is probably true.

"What'll it be, baby?" he asked me, so that he could order for me, telling the waitress, "My associate would like . . ."

My father thinks that's funny.

And maybe it was when I was three. Ha-ha, a three-year-old *associate*.

But that wasn't what I hated. What I hated was that he called me *baby*. Not because it was such an awful nickname, but because I suspect he calls me *baby* when it's too much trouble to remember that my name is Sarah. Sarah, Sarah, Sarah, Sarah, *Sarah!!!!!*

I wasn't always this cranky on our Sunday morning father-daughter outings. I think I was on extra edge this time because sooner or later I was going to have to tell him about my adventures in cheatery.

La.

The waitress brought my father's juice. He took a long drink, then, Ding! Round one, he comes out swinging: "So your mother says you have a tale to tell?"

"Once upon a time," I said in a storytelling tone, "a person brought me a copy of what I hoped were the answers to my geography midterm . . ." (A smiling right hook.)

As he listened, my father nodded and carefully used his knife to push chunks of bagel slopped in gooey egg onto his fork. He *did* look a little surprised to hear that I'd cheated. He peered over his glasses at me, and held his fork up as if he wanted to speak, but then resumed eating and nodded at me to continue.

Overall, he seemed only mildly interested until I got to the part about not telling where I got the test. "You refused the principal?" he asked, perking up.

"I refused the principal on principle," I punned. Then I sat back to wait for the tide. The tide of lawyer-speak. It came right on cue.

My father dabbed his lips with his napkin, leaned toward me, and chuckled, "Ha! Civil contempt! Do you know what that is, baby?"

I shook my head.

"That's having the keys to your jail cell in your own pocket! See, unlike a criminal doing a proscribed block of time, you, my dear, can trade your information for your freedom any time you like."

"But that would be snitching," I reminded him.

"Snitching is official policy in the Army," he said, smiling. "In fact, our own military believes that if you are aware of someone's wrongdoing and you fail to report it, you become as guilty as they are. Therefore, it's a crime *not* to snitch! Grounds for expulsion, in fact."

"Yeah, but I thought it was wimpy to rat on people," I said.

"Well, do we consider the military *wimpy* or *manly* for taking this stance?" My father smiled even more. He loves this kind of conversation.

I hate it.

"The police call it 'The Blue Wall,'" he continued. "The code of silence within the force. One cop never tells on another cop, no matter how corrupt or onerous he or she may be. It's simply not done."

I wondered if my father was telling me that I was being honorable—or the opposite. I tried to keep my foot from shaking impatiently, but when I held my foot still, my fingers started drumming.

Meanwhile, the tide continued. I felt my father's words breeze past without ever touching me. He was talking about the *idea* of tattling, but it wasn't about me or my situation in particular. It was, as always, nothing personal.

As he laughed at one of his own jokes, I finally interrupted to say, "Well, Dad, what do *you* think I should do?"

He raised his palms in a shrug. "Beats me, baby. But it's a very interesting dilemma, I'll give you that!"

> I am a stick of dynamite
> And I feel the end of my personal fuse
> Drawing dangerously near.
> Spark and sputtery
> Bright string on fire!
> Hot!
> Twisting ash-worm eating toward
> KA-BLAMMO!!

No! No explosion. No temper. Not here, not now. I tried hard to control my voice and said, "This *interesting dilemma* is my real life, you know."

He blinked at me, blink, blink. "Yes, of course it is, baby. I know that." Then he glanced down at the orange slice on my plate and said, "You going to eat that?"

When I got home, my mother asked what my father said about my cheating.

I shrugged.

"You didn't tell him?" she asked.

"I told him," I said. "And he thought it was *interesting*."

Mom shrieked, "He *what*?" Then she made a beeline for the telephone to tell her girlfriends about my father's latest blunder.

I went to my room.

Rob

So quiet, I wonder if I'm dead. Then recognize my room, my stuff. It's light out, so why does the clock say eleven? Must've slept through to the next day. Sunday, right?

Pull on pants, unlock door, go downstairs. No one. Not even my kid brother. Turn into the kitchen—father sitting at the table. I think: Here goes.

He says, "Morning."

I say, "Morning." Look around for the trick, a hint of his mood. Nothing out of place or weird.

Get the box of cereal, milk. Pour myself a bowl. Shut the box right—fold the inner bag, put the tab in the slot. Put the milk carton back in the fridge. Go to the table, sit across from him. About to eat when I remember the napkin. Jump and almost topple my chair. Then sit with my napkin. Begin to eat.

Ma comes in with a basket of laundry. Sets it down on the third chair. Starts folding, looking nervous.

Asks me where my backpack is.

My uniform comes home for her to wash on weekends. It's usually in my backpack stinking up my books on Fridays.

"Left it somewhere," I say, remembering that I'd ditched it behind some bush. "I'll get it later."

Ma nods, folding, trusting me still.

Is anyone going to say anything about my being gone all night? About cheating on the exam? This is torture. Starved as I am, the cereal turns to clay in my mouth. Can barely squeeze it down my throat.

Ma's done folding, takes the clothes to the other room. Old man still hasn't said a word since "Morning."

Keep eating but my neck feels creepy. Like he's watching me and waiting. Wish he'd get it over with, but no. Nothing to do but wait. Chew, swallow, and *wait*.

Finish gagging down breakfast. Rinse bowl and spoon, put them in the dishwasher. Wipe the counter trying not to give him *anything* to start about. Even square the sponge with the edge of the sink.

Kid brother bangs through the front door. Feet stampeding this way. Bursts into the kitchen, yells, "Robby!"

Dad freezes him with a growl: "Not now."

Brother says, "But—"

Dad stands.

I'm already standing, I move between them. Turn to the kid, say, "Hey, wazzup?" I put my hand out for skin.

Kid looks from our old man to me, back and forth, getting pale.

Dad sits back down. Turns away.

I un-puff my chest.

Kid nervously slaps me five, shoots panic looks at the old man. Then backs out of the kitchen, thumps down the hall, bangs out the door.

No one speaks till I say, "Guess I'll go get my pack."

And my father says, "Want a lift?"

I don't get it. "A lift, sir?"

"I could take you to get your backpack."

"Oh. Thanks. I mean, you don't have to . . ." Stuttering.

Is he taking me out to murder me, dump my body somewhere? No, that's stupid. But what'll he do when he finds out I'm not sure where my pack is?

He's sort of smiling at me. My gut sinks—the clay-cereal I'd shoved into it hardens to stone.

Jake

Technically, I didn't cheat. I'm not in that class. I'm not even taking geography this semester. So why couldn't I just forget the whole stupid psychodrama and get on with studying for my own midterms?

But I couldn't concentrate. And I must have been acting strange, because my mom, who isn't normally the most perceptive person on the planet, kept feeling my forehead for fever.

She pouted her overly-red lips and said, "You look funny."

"Well, I'm just funny-looking," I snapped back. And she giggled as if that was the joke of the year.

For one hopeless, suicidal moment I considered dumping my whole story on her. I began by saying, "Mom, did you ever cheat in school?"

She giggled some more, of course, and then said, "Don't be silly! What a question! Just because I wasn't as good a student as you or your sister? Maybe no one gave *me* shiny brass plaques and certificates and whatnot. But I was certainly smart enough to pass without cheating!" Then she laughed some more. I tried to get back to work.

Rob

He asks which way. I point north. Woulda liked to set the
odometer, see how far I hiked yesterday. But he'd think I'm
bragging or proud—not sorry enough about the trouble I
caused.

We drive. I sweat, trying to remember where I dumped
that pack.

Out of nowhere he says, "So what do you weigh now?
'Bout one-sixty, one-sixty-five?"

"One-seventy-eight, sir," I answer.

"I've still got thirteen pounds on you," he says. "And don't
forget it."

"No, sir," I say. "I won't." But I wonder what he means.

Finally, way the heck across the San Fernando Valley, I spot
the bush. Don't know how I recognize it.

I say, "Stop here!" He does. I jump out, and the pack's
there. Relief. I get back in.

"You walked all the way here?" he asks.

"Yes, sir."

"Didn't hitchhike?"

"No, sir." Want to add this ain't even *half* as far as I got, but I don't.

When we're almost home he says, "I guess I was about your age when I fought back. Sure must've taken my daddy by surprise." Then he points at me. Says, "Don't even think of it, boy."

I say, "No, sir, I won't."

He pats his gut. "You may think this here's an extra thirteen pounds of flab—nothin' but old man sag and fat. But don't kid yourself."

"No, sir," I say. "I won't."

He nods. Says, "Plenty of scrap and gristle left in the old guy."

I answer, "Yes, sir."

Then I get it: He's scared if he hits me this time, I'll slug him back. And ya know what? He's right. How'd *he* know that before *I* did?

Suddenly it's like tasting that lemonade, still cold, out of the trash. Third jolt: Yes!

You'd think running away woulda told him I was *more* of a coward than ever, *less* of a threat. But he must've just now noticed that I'm bigger than him. Took *me* till now to notice.

Maybe he thinks I'd had enough. Thinks I'd take off again and this time the police wouldn't bring me back.

Maybe so.

He's dead wrong about one thing, though: He doesn't have no extra *thirteen* pounds of flab. More like an extra thirty-five.

I feel myself inflate, fill up the entire car. Feel great.

Then less great: My old man is just an out of shape bully-turned-coward afraid of payback time. I'd dreamed of this, but now that it's here, it almost makes me sad. I practically pity the old guy—but not quite.

Get home. Go to my room. Don't bother to lock the door.

Little brother comes in, asks why everyone's acting all weird.

Tell him about the geography test.

He gets scared for me. "Dad know?"

I say, "Yeah."

"He mad?"

I shrug. "He'll get over it," I say.

My brother looks at me like I'm the biggest, toughest dude in town. I say to him, "Whoever it was said, 'If you ain't cheatin', you ain't tryin' . . ."

My brother nods. Listens hard, like I'm someone.

"Guy's wrong," I say. "He thought if you want something bad enough you'll do whatever it takes to get it. But that's stupid, 'cause then if you get it—it's not *you* who got it. It's some made-up, fake you, and the real you got nothing. Diddly. Zip. Know what I mean?"

My brother nods his head off, but who knows what he got. Then he follows me back down to the kitchen. Watches me eat.

Nothing tastes like clay. I swallow fine.

Sarah

Punishment Poem Continued

I spent the evening overeating,
That was my way of retreating.
I knew that this was self-defeating,
But the guilt was only fleeting.

Then there came a stranger's greeting
And an accidental meeting
Leading to a last-ditch cheating
For which I now receive this beating.

And who is it that's beating me:
My teacher or my family?
Who punishes my villainy?
And remedies this tragedy?

Just me. And my own gluttony,
My personal catastrophe.
There's none to thank and none to spank.
There's no one here but ME.

Monday

Rob

Dig my grungy-looking test out of my pack. Slide it across the breakfast table.

"It's wrong to cheat," Ma whispers.

I say, "I know, Ma."

She looks at me with sad eyes.

"It's not going to happen again," I say. "I swear." Hand her a pen. Point to the red line Mr. Chen drew across the bottom.

"I worry about you," she says.

"No need," I say, and give her a pat.

Then my brother comes, so Ma quickly signs it, pushes it toward me.

"The kid already knows," I tell her.

She sighs.

My old man doesn't show for breakfast. Wonder if he's sleeping off a late night. But Ma says he left early. Had some things to attend to.

Fine, good. It's all good.

Dan

CHEATING ESSAY:

Dear Sirs, Mr. Chen and Mr. White,

I hope you will both accept my apology for the trouble Friday regarding the geology midterm. I have learned my lesson and I will not hang around with people like that anymore.

I hope we can all go on as if nothing happened.

Sincerely,
Daniel Brand

Sarah

How did Mr. Principal even know I was in class? Do the faculty have buzzers under their desks? Walkie-talkies to alert him? Someone must've sounded the alarm, because the second I sat down, his voice broke into class, telling me to report to the office.

Every head turned to look at me.

There
are
no
secrets
here.

It felt much different walking to the office today than it felt on Friday. It's amazing, really, how quickly I got used to being the girl who gets called down by the principal.

When I got to the office, Ms. Gold, the secwetawy, smiled

a sad smile at me and waved me into Mr. Chen's office.

The girls' guidance counselor, Ms. Divan, was already in there. She smiled the exact same sad smile that Ms. Gold had. I know Katie thinks Ms. Divan is divine, but to tell the truth, I don't see why.

"I'm glad to see you've decided to return to school, Sarah," Mr. Principal began. "But you forgot to stop by here before reporting to class."

I said I didn't know I had to.

So he said, "I thought the conditions of your return were spelled out clearly enough. That we simply must have the name of whoever supplied you with last year's exam before we can allow you back in class."

Ms. Divan spoke up using her *understanding* voice. "Sarah, dear," she said. "We are fully aware of the awkwardness of your situation, but please trust that the right thing to do is to tell us what you know."

"And *why* is that the right thing to do?" I asked. I may have asked it in a snotty way, but it was a reasonable question. No one yet had said why tattling was suddenly okay.

Mr. Principal bristled. "As I've told you before, Sarah, this sort of business must be stopped before it takes hold. I simply will not tolerate it! Not at *my* school."

"Mr. Chen, sir," I said. "This was *not* a business transaction. It was a personal favor."

"Some favor!" he sneered.

"Well, it was *meant* as a favor," I said. "And anyone can see that it was *not* a great business scheme. We were caught. It failed."

"We can do without the attitude," he said, and I sighed.

Ms. Divan spoke up. "Don't try to protect anyone, Sarah, dear. Obviously this person does not feel the same kind of loyalty toward you."

She waited for that to sink in, or for me to say something, but I didn't.

We

    both

        waited.

She gave up first and said, "Let me tell you this: It doesn't show a very healthy sense of self-worth for you to cover for someone who'd do something like this to you."

I'd meant to be silent for the rest of this meeting, but I broke down and said, "No one *did* anything to me. He didn't give me an outdated test on *purpose*." (Oops.)

"*He!*" Mr. Principal cheered. "Now we're getting somewhere!"

But we weren't. I shut back up, and after a few more really lame attempts on their part to get me to name names, they finally gave up.

Chen called my mother again, and I was back out on the bench waiting.

Jake

At the beginning of homeroom, the principal's voice came over the intercom, summoning Sarah to his lair. I watched her gather up her things and walk out of the room as if she were marching to the guillotine. She didn't look to either side. She certainly didn't look at *me*. I wonder if she even knew I was there.

As soon as the door closed behind her, the room began to buzz. Mrs. Pintar tried unsuccessfully to regain order.

I heard someone whisper that Sarah wasn't supposed to come back to school until she told Mr. Chen where she'd gotten the answers she'd cheated with last week.

If that was true, then the fact that she *had* returned must mean she'd decided to tell. My name was probably dropping out of her mouth, onto Chen's desk, right this second. I braced myself, every cell in my body on alert, expecting to hear my name—but the intercom was silent. Why?

Maybe everyone knew. Every student, every teacher . . . And

they were all pretending not to, just to see what I'd do. Just to watch me crumble. The anticipation was surreal.

When I walked down the hall between classes, everyone acted normal in front of me. But I could feel—or at least imagine—thousands of eyes on me, watching, waiting, probably hissing and pointing behind my back. I pictured them all filling their pockets with rocks to throw at me later. Stoning me to death for . . . what? What did I do? *Nothing*. But no one would want to hear my side. It was Sarah's word against mine.

Picture this: Beautiful, popular Sarah Collier, goddess of eighth grade, on one side. Me on the other. How fair a trial do you suppose I'd get?

I sat in my next class, so tense that my muscles began to twitch. Still nothing. What was taking our fearless leader so long to call me down to his office? Was he calling in the National Guard for backup in case I went crazy?

This is crazy, I thought. The way I was twisting it all up was out of control. I made myself lean over and ask the girl next to me, a girl named Ashley, if she knew what had happened to Sarah Collier.

Ashley looked surprised. I don't know if it was because I didn't know the latest about Sarah, or because I *did* know anything at all. Maybe she was just surprised that I'd asked her a question. I'd never spoken to her before.

She smiled at me in a friendly way and said, "I heard that Sarah? Was, like, sent home? That she's, like, totally? Suspended?"

Since Ashley spoke entirely in questions, I found myself nodding encouragingly after every word to keep her going.

"And, like, Danielle Bishop?" Ashley said.

Nod.

"Is?"

Nod.

"Going to take Sarah's, like, place?"

Nod.

"On?"

Nod, nod.

"The cheerleading squad?"

"Yes."

Ashley smiled. "At least for the next game?"

Nod.

"Against Wilson?"

My neck was tired and I was stunned. Sarah was doing all this for *me*? Then I cringed. I was letting her? I was hiding behind her? No. I wasn't *hiding*, precisely. Was I?

And was I now thinking in questions like Ashley?

She smiled her perfect white teeth at me.

I hadn't gotten caught. Sarah had. Sarah *chose* to cheat. Sarah *chose* to share the answers with other boys. Sarah got caught. Those are the risks and that's just the way it played out.

Ashley asked if I was all right. I mumbled something and turned away to argue with myself.

Cheating together made us allies, Sarah and me. Even if it included Rob and Dan. I knew that the Hell's Angels had an oath that an attack on *any* one of them was an attack on all. There was no man-to-man, one-on-one fight with an Angel. You tick one of them off, they *all* come and get you.

The members of NATO have the same oath of alliance. That an attack on any one member—France, the UK, Canada, Italy, Norway, etc.—would be considered by each ally as an attack on itself. Each country is expected to fight back accordingly. By that code of honor, an attack on Sarah is an attack on me.

So where did *I* stand? It really irked me that Sarah had shared the test with Rob and Dan, two brainless goons from her crowd. But now it occurred to me to wonder why *they* got off and she didn't. How come *they* weren't in trouble? And then I got it: They sold her out. They blamed her and walked away free. What lowlife cowards!

But what did that make me?

Dan

Rob was in the locker room Monday morning. When I asked why he missed Saturday's practice, he said he'd been on a hike. I don't know if he was kidding or not, but there he was, without a mark on him, so I knew "hike" wasn't another word for "hospital."

I asked him if he'd found out yet who gave Sarah the wrong test, and he shook his head.

"Well, when we do find the creep, we'll have to re-educate him," I said. "Maybe rearrange his face. Can you figure what kind of loser lets a *girl* take his licks?"

But instead of agreeing with me, Rob said that me and him weren't exactly John Wayne when it came to Sarah. He said it like *we* let her take the rap for *us*, but that's not the way it was, man. Not. At. All.

I tried to explain the difference to him. I said, "Sarah isn't any *more* suspended than she would've been if we were suspended *with* her. The only—and I mean *only*—difference is that *we* aren't suspended. See? Either Sarah's suspended *with* us, or Sarah's suspended *without* us. But either way, *Sarah is suspended*. Get it?"

But Rob didn't, or *wouldn't*, get anything. I think my buddy Rob is just nuts. Maybe after all his boo-hooing over how his big bad daddy was gonna nail him, he's embarrassed not to have a single nick in his hide. So now he's into guilt.

But he doesn't have a thing to feel guilty about and neither do I. This is Sarah's deal. Sarah and whoever the dude is.

The truth is, I think there has to be more to this story than meets the eye. Or else why *would* Sarah take the fall for the guy? Especially after he gave her the wrong answers. I figure it this way: She's probably in love with the guy, and he's like a teacher or married, or someone's dad, or some sicko spit like that. Some kinda thing that'll land his sorry butt in jail or cause a scandal with newspaper headlines, right?

I mean, why else would Sarah stay quiet? It doesn't make sense that she'd cover for him if he was just a regular dude.

But Rob said no. He thinks she's doing what she thinks is "right."

"Sure, man," I said. "Like Sarah's such an honest upright citizen! And that's why she got this poor schmo to cheat for her in the first place. Was she just doing what she thought was right when she passed the answers out to the rest of us?"

But Rob wasn't hearing me. He'd gone all hopeless. It just better not screw up his game. That's all I've got to say, and I'm serious.

Anyway, I'd looked around for Ruby before school and between classes. When I found her, though, she gave me the frozen snub. Turned away like I was dirt.

Fine. Forget about it, man. Forget both of them. Sarah, Ruby. There's plenty more chicks out there. Who needs these two loony birds?

Sarah

My mother was a mess. She picked me up from school, again, and said she thought this whole thing was my "desperate cry for help."

She said I'm testing her and she's afraid she's failing the test.

La.

"No, Mother, it's me that failed the test—the geography test."

Ho-ho-ho.

Then she said that:

> It's harder than I think to be a mother alone.
> She did the best she could.
> She hopes I won't repeat her mistakes.
> She hopes I won't marry too young.
> She hopes I won't marry someone like my father.
> Although (she says),
> Daughters *always* do.

So she made an appointment for me to see her psychologist, Rachel-Ann Weisenthal, tomorrow. She said she wants me to have my own therapist, but this is too much of an emergency to shop around for a kid shrink right now.

Kid, schmid. The dreary Ms. Divan is a counselor who supposedly specializes in kids, and she might as well be from Neptune for how well she understands me.

I don't know, maybe my mother's right. Maybe I do need help.

So why doesn't *she* help me? Like she used to help me tie my shoe or reach the sink. How different can this be from shooing bearded gnomes out of my closet at bedtime?

I used to be able to tell her when I was scared. I remember crawling into bed with her when I had bad dreams. She'd kiss my ear too loudly and I'd burrow into her armpit where it was warm and safe. When did that stop?

My mother went back to work, leaving me home alone (la, one lone eon, no?). I stood at the kitchen counter while the TV yabbered commercial after commercial as if they'd forgotten to stick a *program* in there.

I was about to make a tuna sandwich, when my father's newest secretary called. (He goes through them like tissues.) Anyway, I don't know her name and I doubt she even knew she was

> Dialing
> Dad's
> Darling
> Daughter.

She just said, "I have a call for Sarah from Martin Collier."

And I said, "That's me," while turning the TV volume down.

The secretary said, "Go ahead, Mr. Collier," and the next voice I heard was my father's, saying, "I only have a minute, *baby*"—grrrr—"but your mother called me. She is deeply concerned. And while I personally find your position admirable in many ways, I agree with her that this is not an issue worth pursuing at this time. Even *you* must recognize how self-defeating it is. Taken to its logical conclusion, you'd fail the seventh grade—"

I interrupted him to say, "Eighth."

He took a slightly annoyed breath and went on. "You'd fail the *eighth* grade, thereby putting your entire future at risk . . . in exchange for what?"

This was not a question-question. My father did not wait for an answer. He just rolled on. "Perhaps you're too young and hot-headed to evaluate the pros and cons of such a rigid position, but I assure you, you are mistaken if you think it is worth the price."

I replied:

"Your
    concern
    for my happiness
    is really touching."

It was quiet a second, then he said, "Meaning what?"

"Nothing," I answered.

He cleared his throat and said, "So are you going to adjust your stance? In consideration of your future?"

"You mean am I going to go in and tell the principal the

147

name of the kid who gave me the test?" I asked.

My father said, "Well, yes."

I said, "Well, no. I'm not."

A commercial father squatted down and his curly-headed daughter (*I* have curly hair) ran toward him, excited out of her curly skull at the sight of him. I don't know what they were selling, but even with the sound off you could tell she was saying, "Daaaaddy!!!"

"I think you're being unreasonable," my father said.

"I can tell," I answered. My heart was going wild in my chest, but I kept my voice calm.

"Your mother asked me to speak to you about it," he said. I'm sure he'd expected me to blindly obey, as usual. I'd always been sort of a "Yes, sir" kind of daughter.

"And now you've done as she asked," I said. "I'll tell her."

I'd never talked to him like that before. It felt terrible and wonderful and terribly wonderful and wonderfully terrible . . .

Maybe it felt terribly terrible . . .

Or maybe just lonely.

"Well, then," he said. "I'll see you Sunday."

I said, "Okay." And that was that.

> Dead phone in my ear. Hear the
> Hissssss. Not a snake or a leak.
> But a curling flame running a fuse.
> Licking its hot, dry, dynamite lips.
> Wake up and smell the tuna.
> KA-BOOM!!
> Daddy?

148

I stared at my expressionless reflection in the oven door and thought, It's just you and me, kid.

Even *I* couldn't tell from looking at myself that I was scared. How could my face look so calm and normal while I was so confused and terrified inside? Shouldn't it *show*?

Here's the scariest part: My parents thought I knew what I was doing.

How come they thought I was so grown up all of a sudden?

Why did *they*, of all people, fall for this face? Shouldn't they still be able to see through it?

When I was little, my mother used to say she could tell if I was lying by looking at my tongue! And of course I believed her, and of course—she was right. At what age did I learn that as long as I let her see my tongue, she'd believe whatever I said?

I know that it can feel just as *good* as it does *bad* to get away with a lie. But both ways, it's lonely.

Anyway, now my mother didn't ask to see my tongue anymore. She just believed me, I guess. Both of them believed that I knew what I was doing with my life. They thought I knew what I was doing about this Jake thing. They thought it was a bad plan, but the point is, they thought I *had* a plan.

Boy,

were

they

wrong!

I didn't know what I was doing. I knew I didn't want to flunk out of school and become a nothing with no future. And I knew that I didn't give a hoot about Jake.

But those weren't good reasons to give up and give in, were they?

Who could I ask? Who could I even talk to about it?

I was a lone eon on loan to no one. It took my breath away how alone I was.

Katie

When I saw Sarah before school this morning, she said she was sure everything would work out okay. But I could tell she was nervous. She didn't say anything about my new shoes. Not that they're the most important thing in the galaxy, but trust me: If Sarah were herself, she would've noticed them.

Then when she didn't show up for lunch, I panicked. I asked a girl named Brenda (who's in Sarah's class second hour) if she'd seen her. She hadn't.

Then Brenda's friend Ruby told me that she'd heard that Sarah was in the principal's office again!

But I hadn't heard Sarah called over the PA.

One girl, Ashley, who's in Sarah's first hour, said Mr. Chen called her down to the office the minute class started. And when I said I didn't hear the PA, she said, "Sarah? Was, like, SURGICALLY removed?" She wasn't asking me anything. That's just how Ashley talks. Then she said, "Later? I saw

Sarah? Goin' out? Like, to the parking lot? With, like, her, like, sister? Or whatever?"

HUH? Sarah's sister—I mean HALF sister—is only three years old! But then I realized she meant Sarah's MUM. Mrs. Collier is kind of young-looking, especially from a distance.

By then other kids had come up to us. They were all talking about Sarah, saying they'd heard she was suspended. Everyone expected me to know the truth since we're best friends. But all I could do was shrug and shrug.

I went down to the pay phones and called Sarah's house. But Mrs. Collier answered and said she was on the other line and to call back later (click).

I held the phone in my hand and my mind flashed back to when I used to sneak down here to call home. For a while I hoarded coins so I could call whenever I needed to. Some days I called before every class. That's six times a day.

My mum would be at work and our answering machine would be on. It always rang three times, and then my dad's voice would answer, as clear as life. "Please leave a message after the beep," he'd say.

I drank it in like some lost-in-the-desert person dying of thirst.

We never talked about it, but when that machine broke, Mum tried to get another one that used the same kind of tape. She called all the stores, but she couldn't find one. Answering machines are all digital now.

Ms. Divan's office isn't all that far from the phones. I cruised by, but her door was closed. I got a drink of water, then walked past again. After going to the bathroom, I passed by her office a third time. Then I went to my locker and got my sweater before I went back and knocked.

Ms. Divan opened her door and seemed happy to see me. She ALWAYS seems happy to see me. She started making small talk, but I cut her off by saying, "Sarah Collier is my best friend."

She nodded.

"I think she's been suspended," I said.

"Yes, she has," Ms. Divan said. So I guess she'd already heard.

"Well, that's not right, suspending her like that," I said.

"She can come back any time she likes, Katie, dear," Ms. Divan said.

I asked if she meant Sarah could come back in exchange for tattling, and Ms. Divan nodded.

"Well, I really think that's mean," I said. "Don't you?"

Ms. Divan shrugged, then shook her head as if to say that was just the way it was.

So I took a deep breath and said, "Then I'm leaving school, too. And I'm going to stay out however long Sarah does. Until she's brought back WITHOUT having to tattle."

"Katie!" Ms. Divan gasped. "You're threatening to walk out?"

"No, ma'am," I said. "I'm not THREATENING anything. I'm just telling you what I'm going to do."

Ms. Divan's face flushed and she half-stood. "Katie, you'd better think this through!" she said. "I understand and appreciate your loyalty to your friend. And I also appreciate that

153

you're trying to right what you feel to be a wrong. But don't be hasty here. The repercussions could be quite severe!"

I waited for her to say more, so she did. "Katie, dear, you're a sensible girl. Think about it. What good can come of a single-person boycott?"

I got up on rubbery legs and said, "Well, anyway, bye." And I left her office.

She called my name but she didn't come out after me, so I kept walking.

Still shaky, I made my way down the hall and out the front door of the school.

Nothing happened. Jailbreak alarms didn't sound. Snarling attack dogs didn't come at me with their fangs bared. It was amazing really, to realize that nothing held us in school besides the fact that we were supposed to be there.

I'd never thought about it, but I'd always felt there was a force field, an invisible fence, a SOMETHING that kept all of us inside from the first bell to the last. I glanced around for truancy police and almost laughed out loud, thinking of myself as a juvenile delinquent. A criminal. Ha! It was thrilling! No wonder kids skipped school.

Here I was, walking down the school's long driveway. Happy, amazed, blinking in the bright sunlight, illegally ALONE! I felt taller, stronger. My lungs filled with air. Not CLEAN air, of course, but NEW air. Free air!

Rob

CHEATING ESSAY:

Here's why cheating rots. Because it's lying. Because it's trying to pass yourself off as someone else. Also, if people cheated and got away with it, they'd go around acting like they know stuff that they don't know. Pretending to be someone they're not. Then after a while they'd probably believe it themselves.

And even if they got sick of lying all the time, it would be hard to suddenly come clean. To tell people you're a big fake. You might even get thrown in jail. Like if you were a pilot flying planes and you'd cheated on your flight tests. Or you're the guy who fixes the plane but you really don't know your gears from a hole in the ground, so the plane crashes and everyone dies. You're guilty of murder.

If a lot of people cheat, then none of them would be who they say they are. And there'd be no way to know what's really going on. Like to tell which mechanic can fix your plane and which ones'll kill you.

Everyone would be worried about getting caught. They'd be suspicious of everyone else. So all together the whole world would be a drag and everyone would be afraid.

Signed,
Robert King

Katie

When I got to the end of the school driveway and hit the "real" world, I wondered if I should go: A) Home? B) To my mum's office? C) To Sarah's house? Or D) To the coffee shop on the corner. By myself.

That thought made me taller still. If this kept up I'd be as tall as Sarah by dinnertime. I grinned, picturing myself sliding l-o-n-g legs into one of the restaurant booths. I'd order fries and a Coke, or maybe a piece of pie and a cup o' tea. I'd take my books out and do some studying or maybe I'd read.

Girl alone. On her own. Mysterious. Independent. I smiled harder, walking along, picturing it.

Girl alone, protesting the mistreatment of her friend. A boycott of one (as Ms. Divan had dubbed it). I liked the sound of that. But she was right that a one-girl demonstration wouldn't WOW anybody. I'd have to call in some troops, right?

The first person I thought of was Rob. Secretly, he's often the first person I think of. But THIS time it made perfect sense. I'm sure he'd want to help.

A car slowed down and the driver leaned over to peer out the window toward me. I thought he was lost, so I went closer to the curb to offer directions. But then his window went down and he said, "Hey, baby," in a low, slow voice that chilled my blood.

I jumped back onto the sidewalk, picked up my pace, and stared straight ahead. The car moved on, but I didn't slow down until I'd reached Sarah's door.

Boy, was she surprised to see me. So surprised that she threw her arms around me and gave me a hug! That was a first. And guess what she did next? Something else I'd NEVER seen Sarah do before. She cried. Not great snorting floods of tears, but enough to make my shoulder wet.

Then, when I told her that I'd left school in protest, and hoofed it to her place all alone on my own two feet, she stood speechless. Sarah at a loss for words? Talk about FIRSTS!

Rob

Katie called. She's really something else. She's *doing* something about the Sarah thing. I promised to help. We talked easily, like we used to. Had forgotten her catchy laugh. Like being tickled when you're little . . . Can't help yourself, just crack right up.

I call all the guys on the team. Doesn't feel like enough. So get the school directory. Call down the alphabet. More like it.

Call one kid, Jake Broder, who freaks. "Who told you to call *me*?"

"Relax, Bud," I say. "I'm calling everyone. I'm on the B's."

"But why *me*?" he's yelling. "Tell me the truth! Why'd you call *here*?" Tell him what I'm telling everyone: We're boycotting school tomorrow. Showing the administration that we think their treatment of Sarah is wrong.

Hangs up on me—he isn't the only one. Slew of kids whine about midterms, parents.

Ma musta heard. Comes in the den with her hands

clutched. Says, "Haven't you gotten in enough trouble, Robby?"

No time to reassure her. So many calls to make, don't want to miss anyone. By 11:30, talk to—or leave messages for—130 seventh graders, 209 eighth graders. With six wrong numbers and eleven "no English"es, that's the whole middle school.

Lot of kids already know. Say the phone's been ringing all night with the same message. Good! Word's out. Ear burns red from the phone, but feel better than I've felt in days, weeks, months. Willing to bet at least 35, maybe 50 kids boycott tomorrow.

That Katie, she's somethin' else. Always has been.

Ruby

First, I hear about it from Brenda, and I'm all, like, she's making it up or it's, like, a rumor or something. But then the e-mails start in from practically everyone that there's going to be, like, a school *protest*. And I'm all, like, "Oh. My. God. It's all so '60s, hippie-peace-love-flowers! Like, wear your beads and be groovy!"

What a scream! *Everybody's* going to boycott until, like, our school principal—I can never remember his name—lets Sarah Collier come back to school!

My brother-in-law-to-be raises his fist in the air when I tell him, and he's all, like, "Power to the people!" And yelling, "The revolution has come!"

I, like, giggle. But my sister rolls her eyes and she's all, "Gimme a break, Mack." Like he's beyond stupid. She acts annoyed with him *all* the time now. Mom says it's totally normal to hate the groom right before the wedding. But I think it's gross.

Anyway, my sister says she's, like, *"telling"* if I skip school, and that Mom'll kill me. But I go, like, "Get a life, twit. It's got *nothing* to do with you!"

And right then and there, I decide to, like, for sure boycott. Either I'll just cut class and go to the mall with my girls, which would be fun! Or, if no one else is into it, I can always just stay home with, like, cramps or something, and work on my tan. I think this is *so* cool! I'm, like, *loving* this!

Then I get to, like, thinking about it, and I figure Danny of all people should definitely, like, totally boycott tomorrow. Not that I *care*, but still. It's, like, practically the *least* he can do for Sarah, considering he got totally away with everything and she, like, didn't.

I mean, I'm all: He should be feeling guilty, right? And wanting to make it up to her?

Okay, so I call him and he acts like it's no big deal—like I call all the time, and we're still, you know, together or whatever.

So all tough-like, I go, "There's a protest tomorrow."

And he goes, like, "My man Rob told me."

So I go, "You better be boycotting."

And he goes, "Are you?"

And I'm all, "Du-uh."

And he laughs and asks me, like, where I'm gonna spend the boycott day, and I'm all, like, "What's it got to do with you?"

And he laughs, ha, ha, ha, funny. And says maybe he'll stop by my house tomorrow.

And I say, "Maybe I won't be here." And I, like, hang up.

Well, now I'm all: Who knows? I mean, it's not like Ryan, that bass player, has exactly called me or anything. At least, not yet.

But I'll see what Bren and Ashley wanna do tomorrow.

And Danny? I'll think about that later, or, like, *not*.

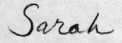

Sarah

....
    Phone to phone.......................
        ear to ear...................................
            the plan weaves........................
                a spreading sticky net...............
                    over our town........................
                    ....

Who would have believed that quiet little Katie could create such a stir? She got the phone lines burning up with her plots and schemes. And she was cackling like a lunatic on the phone with Rob—the two of them hatching their protest plan. Giggling and scheming like little spies.

And I admit, I was amazed—and touched, both by what she was doing and by the kind of reaction she was getting.

164

That Katie Tomatie,
Peach of my eye.
Most other potaties
Would not even try!
What a gal! What a pal!
So true and so blue!
That Katie, ma' lady,
Oh thanka, thank you.

I wasn't tweeked enough to think anyone (besides Katie) was helping because they like me so much. I knew that most of the kids were only interested because it breaks up the school-week boredom. But that's okay. My grandma told me that she was mostly involved in the Peace Movement because that's where all the cute guys were.

But still, who would have guessed that *any* kids at school could get riled up about this? Who'd have believed they'd even care?

It was embarrassing, but nice.

Very nice.

Jake

Well, that sure was a prime example of what can happen if you're popular and beautiful: The entire student body makes *your* problems *their* problems. You become their cause, their damsel in distress, and they become chivalrous and noble just by defending you. Needless to say, whatever you did to get in trouble in the first place is forgiven and forgotten.

If I or any other nerd-like student was in Sarah's position? How fast do you think the other students would have rushed to help me/us? If I, or someone like me, got suspended, we'd rot. The Sarahs land on their feet—I land on my ass.

But here was my question: Was I supposed to boycott, too? Would that erase some of my guilt?

Guilt? Was I suffering from guilt?

Well, every now and then I let a corner of my mind toy with the idea of going to the principal's office and turning myself in as the missing link. The mystery man. The one Sarah Collier was protecting. But then what? I'd be suspended.

Half the guys in love with Sarah would probably jump me and beat me to a pulp in an attempt to impress her. And who would object? *No one.* No one would defend *me.* No one was going to boycott in *my* name.

And so much time had passed that now I wouldn't get *credit* for coming forth—only *blame* for having waited so long! I couldn't win. There was no way.

I wished my uncle were around. I'd ask him.

Meanwhile, what would I do *tomorrow*? Would it be hypocritical of me to boycott? And what did they mean by "boycott"? Marching around in front of the building carrying signs and yelling slogans through megaphones? Or just skipping school and staying home watching game shows?

This was making my head spin. I *wished* I'd never given Sarah that stupid test. I wished she hadn't sat next to me in the library. I wished I'd never even met her.

Actually, I wished I'd never been born. Death was always an option. No. No, it wasn't. I had to believe my uncle, that if I got through these years, I'd be fine. I'd get my turn. My day would come.

I reminded myself that someday I'd return for my reunion and there would be Sarah, fat, wrinkled, worn out, with too much makeup and a sloppy, has-been, loser husband. She would look at my custom-made suit, my expensive shoes, my private-yacht tan, my successful face, my amazing car, my gorgeous blond wife, and she'd think . . .

Hey, Mr. Chen was probably going to suspend everyone who boycotted tomorrow. He pretty much had to. It was a power thing. I was positive he'd think he had to act tough so we don't start boycotting left and right, demanding things like edible lunches or better computer access, or teachers who actually know something about the subjects they teach.

I got the phone book down to look up his home number. Kevin B. Chen. It was ridiculously easy. I wondered if he got hounded at home by students all the time. I'd have an unlisted number if I was him.

I dialed. A woman answered. A wife? A daughter? Mother? Housekeeper? She called him to the phone.

He said "Yes?" instead of hello.

I didn't tell him my name. But I told him I had some information that he was interested in. He asked if this was some kind of joke. I said no. I asked if it was true that Sarah Collier's punishment would end as soon as the person who supplied her with the test was named. He said he wasn't interested in random accusations. "I need to know the *correct* name of the *actual* person," he said.

I explained that the person he was interested in was me. Then I said I'd tell him all about it, and give him my name, in exchange for a promise.

He stuttered and blustered but didn't promise.

I told him that a bunch of students were going to boycott his school tomorrow. He didn't gasp. I'd hoped he would. I told him *why* they were boycotting. Then I told him that if he swore on his word of honor that he wouldn't punish *any* of them for boycotting, I would turn myself in.

"This is blackmail," he said.

I said, "Actually, it's funny that you should say that, because that's *precisely* what the boycotting students are accusing *you* of. They say *you* are blackmailing Sarah Collier."

He grunted.

I asked if that was a grunt of agreement. I told him I knew that he could pretend this call never took place, that he could go ahead and suspend the boycotters and it would be his word against mine. But I reminded him that *he and I* would know the truth. "Plus, I'm taping this call, of course," I said, which wasn't strictly true.

He grunted again. Which I suspected was as close as I was going to get to a promise.

So I told him my name. And he sounded surprised to learn that I was me. Then I told him that I stole the test from my sister Beth. He remembered her, of course. She was probably the best student he ever had in his school.

I hung up.

I stared at the phone. Had I *done* something here? Was it brave or cowardly? I had hot flashes and cold chills. Fear—relief. Fear—relief. My hands were freezing and soaked with sweat. I had done something.

Epilogue

Dan

So it was Jake Broder! That's a shocker, man. Jake is one of the smart kids. I never would've figured him to get mixed up like this. Then again, who can blame the guy?

Imagine him, just living his little nerd life, minding his own pathetic nerd business with a cool factor of zero, when along comes *Sarah Collier*, man—looking the way she looks. Looking that way *at him*. He probably didn't know what hit him. Must've thought he'd died and gone to heaven. Poor sucker didn't stand a chance.

Maybe she'd leaned against his locker and smiled that smile of hers. Maybe she did that thing where she rubs the ankle of one foot with the toe of the other. Who wouldn't give her their sister's old test? Who wouldn't give her their eyeteeth?

I didn't blame the dude, not in the least. And I bet there wasn't another guy in this whole school who did either.

Chicks. The garbage they get us to do. It's nuts, man. Just nuts.

Ruby

I go, "*Jake Broder???*"

And Brenda's all, like, "I know!"

And I go, "He's in my science class or, like, history or something, and I never thought he was all that, you know, whatever."

And Brenda says, "I know."

And I'm still, like, amazed, so I go, "Can you believe *Sarah Collier* has, like, the *hots* for him? She could have any guy!"

So Bren goes, "I know!"

And I say, "I've never even *seen* them together, like, *ever*—Sarah and Jake. What's up with that?"

Bren nods and says, "I dunno."

Then Ashley, who has been quiet as a mouse till now, goes, "I personally? Have always, like, thought? Jake Broder? Was kinda cute."

"Aw, get outta here," I say. "You're totally lying."

"Through your caps," Brenda agrees.

But Ashley says, "I swear? And I do not? Have, like, a single? Speck of trouble? Seeing why Sarah? Was, like, trying? To protect him."

I roll my eyes and go "Fttttt" to Bren.

And Bren goes "Fttttt" back at me and says, "I know."

But Ashley says she's totally serious, and she goes, "Do you think I care? Like, what *you* say? Well? I don't. And when Sarah's? Done with him? I have, like, every intention? Of asking that boy out."

So Brenda goes, "Gross!" and we both lose it. But not only does Ashley not crack up, she, like, doesn't even crack a smile! Alls I've got to say is: "Look out, Jake!"

Jake

My four-day suspension ended yesterday, and I was *not* look-ing forward to returning to school. I didn't know what to expect. Would I get jumped and pulverized by an angry mob? Or attacked by individual thugs who had put their names on the official beat-up-Jake-Broder sign-up sheet? At best, I pic-tured myself being shunned and ignored.

But *never* did I imagine being waved to and smiled at and helloed by so many kids. It was remarkable. Sarah just gave me a fraction of a nod, but Ashley, that girl from my second-hour class, took my arm and smiled up into my face and told me she thought I was *terrific*. How about that?